Six Spears

of the

haebinnor

by Frank J. Perricone

illustrated by the author

Table of Contents

Chapter 1: Sand In Their Breath

"Keep your trouble to yourself, and the whipping that's sure to follow," Yaletha protested. She was a thin slip of a girl, easily overlooked. Though the work she did for her master was strenuous -- at this moment, she was wringing out his horse's dressing, having just beaten the dust and sand out of it -- she seemed never to put on any muscle. If she drew herself to her full height and a proud posture, she would have been striking, even pleasing to the eyes, despite her slim form. But this was something she never did. She preferred to crouch and be overlooked. Those who were overlooked were rarely punished.

"It's not my trouble. It belongs to Thargoz, and to all of the Haebinnor!" Yaletha was unswayed; Jemik always thought whatever was happening was of the utmost urgency, and even more so, that it was time to act. Jemik liked to take action. It was far easier than thinking, particularly for him. What Yaletha wondered is why he seemed so determined to involve her in his schemes. Kumza would insist that it's because Jemik fancied her, or "has an eye for you," as Kumza would put it, but Yaletha doubted this. Or perhaps just hoped it wasn't true. There seemed little point in fancying or being fancied; the Haebinnor were slaves to the last, and had no rights to choose for themselves. The whole idea of romance seemed like yet another means of getting into trouble. Anyhow, Jemik ought to fancy Oyana instead, Yaletha reasoned. She was like him, tall, strong, and fierce. Well, not entirely like him. She was cunning, and had a keen eye. Yaletha reasoned she was what he needed to balance out his rash and thoughtless ways.

With a sigh, Yaletha passed one end of the horse-blanket to Jemik, and without even thinking, he held it and braced himself while she began to twist it once more. Beneath, a large pan caught most of the drippings wrung from the cloth, which would be used to clean other things, to water horses, or, if it had become too foul even for that, would be given to Yaletha and the other slaves of the house to drink. No water could be spared here. Farther north or west, nearer the Inland Sea, the land was fertile and the springs and streams generous. They had great crop-lands and deep rivers, and terraces atop which grew grapes which they made into the strongest wine for hundreds of leagues, or so Jemik claimed to have heard. Yaletha had never seen grapes, nor a river, let alone a sea, and could imagine none of them.

"Thargoz is a fool, and so are you to believe these rumors. The Six Spears tell us that we must be wary of false signs. If people act too quickly, the Oritheri will be ready when..." She paused in wringing and leaned a bit closer to whisper. "When the day comes for the Haebinnor to rise. If this were the First Spear, which it cannot be, there would be time to find out without taking rash action. By stirring up others, Thargoz isn't just putting himself in danger, and those who know him and may be punished with him; he's endangering all of the Haebinnor. Should we act too soon, or reveal the prophecy, *the Haebinnor shall fall, sand in their breath, and perish unto the last child, to the end of days.*"

Despite himself, Jemik was mouthing these same words as she spoke them. Every child of the Haebinnor learned every word of the Six Spears at a young age, even before they could understand them. It was safer to pass this secret knowledge to them very early; if they waited until the child was older, the Oritheri might overhear, or the child might be taken away before the lesson could be taught. That was a dread fate, indeed. Every Haebinnor child had before him a lifetime of servitude, of punishment and poverty, being passed from one owner to another like kine, hoping only to escape the cruelest of masters. There was nothing to sustain one in this life, save the foretelling in the Six Spears. *A day will come.* Four words, the first four in the prophecy, muttered under the breath in times of tribulation and pain, could sustain any of the Haebinnor. They were an incantation of hope. But the Six Spears also spoke warnings. A wiser man than Jemik might, when driven to take action in anger or haste, murmur another incantation: *sand in their breath*, as a talisman of reserve. If a day will come, every Haebinnor must wait for it, patiently.

2

But Jemik was neither wise nor patient. "He's being brought to the well, but the Oritheri Dond doesn't know who broke the vase yet. And with so many of the warriors gone away to join the siege of the Kingdom of the Sea-Lords, many places go unwatched. I have a plan. If we..." But he trailed off. Yaletha was not arguing with him; that was not her way. Even when she was drawing a line in the sand and refusing him, she did so quietly, meekly. She had turned her back on him, ostensibly to squeeze a few more drops out of the blanket; but in so doing, she had made as clear a statement as she ever would that she would have nothing to do with his plan. Sighing, he said, "You don't wish for trouble. I understand. One day, trouble is going to find you, and having no experience with it, you won't know how to grapple it." But she wasn't listening. He looped his end of the blanket on a nearby post, then turned to stalk off, his gray eyes flashing with ire.

Chapter 2: The First Spear

But Yaletha was not to have the peace she wished for that day.

She had much work awaiting her, and the sun would find slumber long before she did. She would at last climb into a niche carved into a sandstone wall, with more than a dozen of her fellow slaves all around her, many in their own niches. But even in the night, some would be at work; the courtyard that was their home and workspace was never quiet. The sounds would help lull her into dreams, in which the First Hand would rise; she would watch from a safe, quiet distance as he blazed a path to freedom, finally casting the Sixth Spear to the sky. When their chains were cast off, only then would she emerge from her hiding place to join her people in freedom.

And when she awoke, awash in the memories of this dream, she would be filled with guilt at its selfishness. For it had been the lot of scores of generations before her to toil in silence, timidly suffering, merely in hopes that someday one of their children's children's children might see the Six Spears and be free. To hope it to happen in her lifetime, that it might be her and not one of her grandchildren to see freedom, seemed inexcusably greedy.

But before she could have, then regret, this dream, there were many hides to be tanned, and meat to be trimmed and readied for the cooks, and water to be fetched from the well, and much more besides. The day before, her master had gone on a hunt. As was often the case, she had ridden one of his swifter horses, dodging into the small herd of aurochs they found on the plains, then subtly guiding its movement to separate one or two from the rest, so he and his archers could fell the beasts without their bodies being trampled, ruining the hides. It had been a good hunt; he'd even allowed her first pick of the meat from one of them, so pleased was he with her riding, and her finesse at guiding the great beasts.

But that meant the stack of aurochs hides she had to tan was as high as her forehead. As she scraped and pulled at one pelt, she could hear the distant sounds of people milling in the dusty Court of

5

the Well, and she frowned; ire grew within her, though little hint of it would have been seen on her face, even if any had been there to see it. Fools. Thargoz will be beaten until even Kumza's herbs cannot erase the bruises, and likely Jemik with him, and how many others? Why could they not see what had been before them their whole lives? Why could they not remain quiet like a sand-mouse and let the lynx slumber? As she turned to another hide from the stack, she paused to listen. By now, wiser minds should have prevailed, but if anything, it seemed the Court had become more crowded, more restless.

She had shrugged and started scraping at the hide, with perhaps a bit more force than was usual, but only a few beats of her heart measured the space before Ulgi blundered into the courtyard. "Come," he said in his low, guttural voice. "Kumza say come." He beckoned with one hand the size of a cook-pan; behind him, eddies of dust swirled, swept into the air by the vast bulk of his passing.

Yaletha's voice was tender, as it always was when she spoke to Ulgi. "No, I have work to do." She could see, in the eyes of this simple brute, a kindness that few others recognized. And something more, that she couldn't put her finger on. She wondered if even Kumza, whose emotion ran so deep she seemed only to feel rather than to see, knew what was within Ulgi's spirit. There must be something that made her choose to become his mate, but while Kumza could hardly be dissuaded from whispering about romances that Yaletha wished not for, she shared no insights about her own.

At first it seemed Ulgi would accept her refusal. Had Kumza given him something more to say, he would be laboring to remember it, his lips moving silently, but he just stood there. Yaletha turned back to her work, only to be interrupted a moment later as the great brute simply lifted her like a sack of palm-fruits and started to carry her out. Her protests were ignored. "Kumza say must come. If no, bring." She railed, even pounded her small fists on his back, though she wondered if he could even feel it.

6

The hubbub of the Court of the Well grew louder as he carried her towards it, as she'd feared. But as they reached the dusty plaza, the sounds died away. She found herself being placed gently down to meet the gazes of nearly three dozen silent Haebinnor, all staring at her, as if expecting her to speak. Or, from the gape-mouthed way they stared, perhaps they expected her to flap her arms and fly into the sky.

Silence. Dust swirled, and the rope that hung into the well creaked, but the Court remained quiet. She gazed out over them, waiting for someone to speak. As always her eyes recoiled from the sights of the horrors visited upon them. Here, an older woman bent over, her frame weakened with disease; not even Kumza knew how to treat the consumption from spoiled food and tainted water. There, cruel lash-marks had been wound around a young boy's leg, biting so deep that he could no longer walk save with a limp; the Oritheri that owned him didn't care that this made him incapable of work, for there were always new slaves to be bought. Everywhere her eye fell, she saw the signs of misery, and she had to stare at the stones instead, hoping someone might stand up to stop it. But not today. Not here. And certainly not her.

At last, she could not bear the silence. "Why are you all here? Do you know not that the Oritheri Cowr himself is to visit our horse-market this very day? Go back to your dwellings in silence before the lynx awakens!" But the slaves in the Court made no answer. At the far side of the Court she saw Ulgi taking Kumza's hand; near them were Oyana, Jemik, and Thargoz, which meant that Jemik's plan must have worked, whatever it was. They too were staring at her; if anything, her friends seemed even more awe-struck at the sight of her than the other slaves whose names she knew not. "Go back, quietly!" she said once more, trying to catch Kumza's eye, and failing.

"Did you butcher the Oritheri Cowr's horse?" These words came slowly, interrupted by coughs; the disease-wracked woman had taken a few steps closer, holding a horse-hide in her gnarled, bent fingers as she cast the words like stones at Yaletha.

7

The question left her agape. Was she being accused of some wrongdoing? She flinched, fearing punishment, and even more, fearing how this misdeed might fall upon her brethren. But the hue of the hide in the crone's hands caught her eye. "I did," she said slowly as recollection crept into her thoughts. This confession elicited another hush from the crowd. Quickly, she protested, "The horse was lame, and old. The Oritheri Cowr had brought it here and sold it to my master; this is why he is to be here today, buying a new horse. My master bade me to butcher it and prepare the meat..."

Her voice trailed off as she noticed that the wide-eyed stares, which lashed at her like sandstorms on bare skin, were not accusatory. They were something she'd never seen before, could not name, but no less unwelcome for that. She would much rather not be noticed at all, but if she must, definitely not with these rapt, almost awestruck, eyes. "What? What is it?" she asked, her heart racing, her hands shaking.

"The First Hand!" the young boy said, pointing to her.

She started to whirl around to see who was behind her, but there wasn't room for someone to stand there, as she had, habitually, backed up while speaking until the wall had come up against her. It seemed that words themselves hid from her, for she could find none to say. The ailing woman had taken two steps closer, then turned the pelt around, showing the inner surface, where the horse's thews had been cut away to be stewed.

The hide of any beast, and especially a beast of burden, bears markings and whorls, striations and patterns, that arise from the way the beast moves, happenstances of its life, and whatever whims nature itself took in shaping skin and muscle. The skins clearest and plainest were saved for parchment, but far more had grains and lines that made them better suited to other uses. This hide showed many discolorations and splotches, which was no surprise. The horse had been ridden by the Oritheri Cowr for at least six years, and had before that come to his hand from a merchant trader who claimed to have brought the horse from a faraway land. Of course it

8

had markings; a life like that would not result in a pristine, pale sheet.

And of course it had been her who had butchered the beast. That was one of the tasks always assigned to her, and everyone knew it, so why had they asked? Ignoring the boy's pointing finger, she protested, with a hint of ire in her voice, "Why do you bother me with this? I have many more hides of the like to tan this day."

But then her eyes betrayed her voice into silence, for at last, the hide, rotated in the old woman's hands, revealed to her what had brought these people together. There, amongst the natural whorls and lines of the hide, a pattern could be seen. A spear, within a circle. They were only darkenings and creases in the natural hide, formed not by the hand of man but by nature itself; but the image was unmistakable in its likeness.

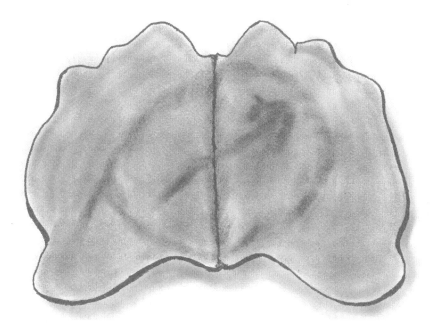

The crone was intoning, and behind her, the others murmured the same words in time. Even Yaletha, having recited them under the sun of a thousand mornings, couldn't help follow along. *"The First Hand shall fell, trembling, a beast of noble blood, within whose very*

9

flesh will be scribed a spear circled; and thus shall the First Spear be seen, and the First Hand known." And into the silence that followed, the old woman pointed at Yaletha, and repeated the boy's declaration: "The First Hand."

The sky seemed to spin, and the Well threatened to hurl itself up over her and cast her to the stones. Yaletha turned and ran, as fast as bare feet on sand could carry her, away from the Court of the Well, away from this impossible portent. This burden must fall to another. She could sense soft footsteps behind her, hear Kumza's voice calling for her, but she fled, heedless, without a thought to where she went, just wishing to be as far from that hide as she could. As far from the truth, grown in the sinews of a horse, as she could run.

Chapter 3: Council of the First Hand

It wasn't often that Yaletha was involved in arguments; she'd made it her life's work to avoid such things. But she had noticed that, when it did happen, inevitably Thargoz and Jemik ended up taking opposite views. They might start from the same place, as they had this time; in fact, all of her friends were enthusiastic that she take up the mantle of the First Hand, no matter how absurd and impossible that was. As the sun sank, Jemik became more determined that she should immediately proclaim herself and lead the Haebinnor to storm Lithgweth. Oyana had to kick him to silence him, lest some Oritheri notice them huddling in a barn in the horse market discussing rebellion, instead of doing their day's work.

Noticing how Jemik's fervor made Yaletha increasingly uncomfortable, Thargoz took a more reassuring tone, and even tried to set a hand on her shoulder to comfort her. He still was convinced by the portent, but he drifted towards a gentler approach. "If Fate has selected you, it must have done so for a reason," he reassured her. "Either because your caution is what is needed, or because when the time comes for you to act it will be at time when you are ready to." She was not reassured, and brushed his hand away, but some part of her appreciated that he'd at least tried.

Meanwhile, Jemik was planning the uprising, or at least he seemed to think so. While he was full of fire and determination, the nearest he got to a true plan was being sure they should set out now. It fell to Oyana to bring some sense to the discussion. There was something about her calm certainty that proved more compelling than Jemik's brash gesticulations; even Yaletha emerged from her near-panic to listen. "Whatever Fate has in mind, there are several more Spears to be seen before the First Hand must act. What we must do for now is to remain calm, and try to go unnoticed, but to keep near to one another. We have known each other a long time." She nodded to Kumza, the one who'd brought this group of friends together. "We can trust one another. We must remain close to protect one another, while we wait to see if the Second Spear is seen. And otherwise go about our lives as usual. Each of us has work to be done before nightfall, lest we meet the lash."

Though even Jemik could see the wisdom in Oyana's words, he couldn't help challenging her authority. "But the Second Spear! How can we be sure, if we don't go to the bogs? What if no one is there? For all we know, it's happening right now!"

"Don't be absurd," Oyana said, "the moon is not arisen."

"But if we don't leave soon we won't be there in time to see it rise!" Jemik protested. *"From mud clinging shall grow the living Second Spear, straining for the bleeding moon.* There was a sandstorm in the east yesternight, so the moon will likely be red this night."

"It will take more than one night for a tree to grow from the bog," Oyana protested. "We cannot stay there watching that long."

For the first time, Yaletha saw fit to speak, her voice shaking. "Yes, the Second Spear will take time. There's no need to rush into anything. Let us go back to our lives and this may all yet come to naught. I will count this day less of a nightmare if only I can escape the lash's caress."

It seemed the discussion had run its course, and while it was plain from the look on his face that Jemik wasn't happy with the outcome, even he could see the consensus that had arisen. Ulgi and Kumza left together, after Kumza had given Yaletha an encouraging hug; then the others filed out one by one, to avoid drawing attention. "I will go with you," Thargoz offered, then added, "to be sure you arrive safely." Yaletha conceded with a slight nod of her head, mostly because she was too exhausted to argue. Night was about to fall, and she had much work still ahead of her.

Chapter 4: Axes In The Dark

The moon shed little light; as Jemik had foreseen, its face was ruddy, the reddish-brown of drying blood, as a result of the dust that hung still in the air. But Yaletha and Thargoz could find their way through the horse-market and back to the work-yard with their eyes closed, and silently besides. If Yaletha were making her way for her sleeping niche, she would have needed no light at all, but she feared the punishment that would follow if she didn't get a few more hides tanned, so, with Thargoz still close by, she found and lit a candle on the bench where she worked. There, her tools still waited where she'd left them.

Well, not exactly. As Thargoz was turning to leave, she found herself staring at her workbench. "What is all this?" Thargoz paused, then took a few steps back as Yaletha circled the table. "These tools aren't mine, and I don't know their purpose."

It seemed someone had added a number of items to the table. There were small clay pots filled with muddy dyes in shades of dark brown, horsehair brushes as might be used in painting, and rough stones, all mingled amongst the scraping-stones, knives, and stretching-racks she used in preparing hides. Not just haphazardly, but placed just so, as if one hand used all of these tools and arrayed them for the work.

Thargoz leaned over the table in the flickering candlelight and twirled that one lock of hair that always hung loose on his forehead. "Are you sure they're not yours? Perhaps you forgot what you were working on earlier. It has been a day filled with distractions."

"Certainly not," Yaletha insisted with surprising certainty. "I've no use for brushes; I only prepare the hides, I do not adorn them. Nor for these… what are they, dyes? What would be the value of dye that's the same color as the natural grains in the…" She trailed off, realization slowly creeping into her eyes.

Thargoz took another moment to come to the same conclusion. "Someone wishes it to look like you've falsified the First Spear," he said breathlessly. Then, a moment later, "Unless... you didn't, did you? No, of course not," he hastily added, before she could object. "But who would do such a thing? No one even knows of the prophecy but the Haebinnor, nor did any Oritheri see the First Spear, so it must be one of the Haebinnor, but who would stand in the way of the prophecy itself? It is our only hope!"

He might have gone on longer, as was his way when he was puzzling something out, had it not been for Yaletha's silence. She had turned around, and was now staring, dumbstruck. He turned and stepped closer to make out what she was gaping at in the dim candlelight.

There was a noose hanging from the rafter beams. An empty noose.

And then, looming out of the shadows, four men, hooded and cloaked, moving to step around them. There were no identifying marks about them, nothing to say who they were. They could have stepped out into the street and vanished, and no one would know who had been there, or indeed that anyone had. But when one spoke, Thargoz felt almost sure that it was an Oritheri voice. No one he could place. No one he'd ever heard before. But there was something in the intonation that suggested the kind of assurance, knowing his place in the world and relishing it, that no Haebinnor, not even Jemik, quite matched.

"Your friends need not be harmed, if you'll make this easy," the hooded figure said directly to Yaletha, gesturing with the blade of a war-axe towards the noose. "It will be quick and the pain, I'm told, is brief. And then all this will be over. No one else will need to suffer, and nothing else will be asked of you."

The man hadn't yet seen Thargoz, he discerned, so he silently moved back a step to keep it that way.

Yaletha stared at the hooded man as she slowly realized what he was suggesting. They'd staged the room so it would look like she'd falsified the First Spear. Then, if the Haebinnor found her the next morning, having hung herself, everyone would be sure she'd taken her own life out of guilt or regret over what she'd done. Perhaps she had done it on a whim, then been taken aback by how much pressure was suddenly on her. People would wonder why, wonder what had been in her thoughts, but no one would doubt it.

And then they'd go back to meekly obeying their masters and waiting for the First Spear. And the Oritheri would have peace again.

Or could it be the Haebinnor doing this? Perhaps there were some who did not wish for freedom. Or more simply, that did not wish for the strife that would come of rebellion. Many of the Haebinnor would suffer and die, before the Sixth Spear was raised and the battle won. Could some of them prefer to remain in comfortable slavery? The idea seemed abhorrent to her, and yet, she wondered. What if she had a safe life in the house of a wealthy master, warm food and a soft bed, easy chores? She'd heard of some who had such lives. Thargoz, for instance, had a life some of her friends sometimes envied.

Or, what if she had a mate? She could not say husband; the Haebinnor had no rights to engage in such a ceremony. But the Oritheri often allowed pairs to stay together, as Kumza and Ulgi did. They turned a blind eye, perhaps because it led to more Haebinnor who could be sold. What if she and another were in love, what if she were carrying a child? Might she favor putting off the prophecy rather than risk her child in the coming struggles?

Betrayal was always a possibility; history was clear on that point. And, after all, the only ones who knew of the sighting of the First Spear, or indeed, who knew the prophecy at all, were the Haebinnor.

In the shadows, Thargoz watched Yaletha closely, and could see in the slightest shifts of her posture how she progressed to darker and darker thoughts. Slumping, frightened, defeated, and surely considering their offer, their threat. Not even Kumza realized how closely he'd been watching her for years; he knew the way the

15

sunlight kissed her olive skin, every curl in her dark hair, every wrinkle on her slender fingers; and more than these, he knew how the cast of her eyes and slant of her shoulders spoke volumes she would never say aloud about the shifting of her moods. He saw how quick she was to hide from responsibility or conflict, but he also suspected inside her a simmering anger that she suppressed with her conciliatory tone. And the way she stood now, the half-step she took, the shake in her hands, told him that she was losing this battle of wills. She would give her life to protect her friends, but more, to avoid the terrible burden of prophecy that had placed itself on her shoulders. If she put her neck in the noose, it would fall to someone else to save her people, and she would be free, not of her chains, but of expectations.

There were four of them, but Thargoz had the element of surprise. They hadn't expected anyone to come back with her, and they didn't know he was there. From the way they moved, it seemed they were less familiar with this particular courtyard than he was; they chose their steps carefully to avoid stumbling over loose cobblestones that he could find with his eyes closed. In one motion, before they could react, he'd snatched a length of timber from one of the tables and run headlong to clip one of the men on his side, causing him to spin into another, bringing them both down in a jumble of cloaks and flailing arms. Another cowled figure took a blow from the timber to the back of his head, and staggered forward, his axe clanging noisily to the stones. The fourth swung his axe skillfully; had Thargoz not been holding the timber, the axe would have caught him in the gut and likely split him wide open. As it was, it bit deep into the wood, shoving the timber from his hands and into his stomach, knocking the wind out of him; Thargoz went down in a silent crumple, but the man lost his axe in the process.

In the moment of stillness that followed, Thargoz could only wait for the inevitable axe-blow as he wondered what he'd been thinking. He couldn't keep Yaletha safe even while his head was still attached, let alone after it was struck off; and what she had to do now would be even harder for her after having to watch him be slain. Perhaps he should have withdrawn to warn the others, or at least to make sure that, when the grisly scene was discovered in the first light of morning, there would be someone who could speak the truth of Yaletha's innocence. Now, they'd find her body hanging from a noose, and his would likely be dumped in parts out in the bog, and no one would know what had happened.

But when the axe came, it didn't find his neck, but instead, his hands. The weapon that had fallen a moment earlier landed at Yaletha's feet, and she'd kicked it to skitter across the cobblestones towards him. He gripped it with shaking hands and used it to push his way to his feet. The fourth cowled figure now found himself unarmed and facing a man with an axe; whatever had brought him here was not something he was willing to die for, and he turned and vanished into the night. Which was lucky; while Thargoz had managed to get to his feet, he didn't have enough breath back to actually swing the axe, but his foe hadn't known that.

"We need to run," he said, letting the axe sink to the stones once more. Of the three remaining men, two were starting to stir. He took Yaletha's hand and pulled, and as he expected, she followed because it was easier than arguing with him.

At least for a moment. As they came to the place where the courtyard opened onto a narrow street, she paused. "But this makes me a runaway. I will never be able to return."

"Those men were prepared to see you dead, by your hand or their own. That spring is already dry, Yaletha. Come, we must find the others and get them to safety before more like these," he gestured towards the men behind him starting to rise, "find them." He tightened his grip on her hand and led her into an uncertain future.

Chapter 5: The Second Spear

That her old life was over, and she could never go back, was not something Yaletha could realize all at once. It hit her like a sandstorm, coaxing tears from her eyes and forcing her to her knees as the weight of it pounded down on her. Then one of her friends would take her hand and guide her through the storm, and she would think she was past it, that the truth of it had worked its way into her like grit into an open wound, where it would become forever after part of her, grinding and grating against her heart.

Then there would be a few minutes of rushing blindly through the wilderness outside the city, heedless of where she was going. Somewhere nearby were their pursuers, those Oritheri whose duty was chasing down runaway slaves. Thargoz had considered it fortunate that he and Yaletha had reached the other four without being spotted by such Oritheri; but there'd never been any chance to get all six of them out of the city without being seen. They hadn't even been out of sight of the towers when the alarm horn had been winded.

Since then Yaletha had run without thought; the grinding of sand against her heart drowned out everything else. Jemik might guide her behind a thorn-bush, or Oyana might choose a path by the light of the blood-stained moon, or Thargoz might whisper to her from around a stony outcropping, and off she would go, trusting them, and too heart-sick to make any other choice. And once they'd found a moment of relative safety, a chance to catch their breath, sand would swirl and come crashing down on her once more, the full weight of realization pressing her to the dusty ground.

If she had had to do this alone, she could not have made it this far. In fact, she would never have run. She would have stepped into the noose and been done with it. Or if she had run, after but a few moments she would turn around and throw herself into the hands of the slave-chasers, take her punishment, and hope she might get to return to her old life, to wait for someone more brave and more capable to lead her to freedom. Or she would curl up under a rock and wait to die of thirst, which is what she wished to do now.

Her five friends were both a blessing and a burden. They kept her going, and gave her direction, towards what she could not even begin to ask herself, but at least away from danger. They made decisions so she would not have to. But if the ending of her old life was too much to bear, how much more so that five others, people for whom she cared, had given up theirs, willingly, to protect her. This was too large an idea to imagine, let alone accept. She had vague memories of a huddled, panicked council in a narrow alleyway, Thargoz retelling the tale of the four cowled men, speculations that all of them would be the next to meet axes in the dark. Hurried speeches about the Spears, about hope, about destiny. Embraces that were meant to be comforting, and kind words about friendship and loyalty that she probably should have been, should be, grateful for, if she had enough life in her to light the spark of gratitude.

But her heart was heavy with the grinding sand of loss. Behind her, a life, terrible and fragile but in its way reassuringly predictable, that was lost forever. Before her, a yawning emptiness of uncertainty. And hanging in the moment between, a slowly swaying noose. The line and loop of rope somehow looked like a spear and circle, folds and grain in hide, a portent of doom. She knew it was supposed to be hope, but she felt it choking her.

The first sign that they'd come far was mud on her foot. Thick, clinging muck, greedy, grasping. She looked up and found her friends standing in an uneven line, all eyes ahead. Above them, the moon was heavy with crimson effulgence, swollen and bloated like a wound, angry and hot. Its ruddy light washed over the damp-slicked hillocks of the bog, making it seem as if blood had been spilled over every mound of damp earth, as if some great battle had been lost here and the moisture was life itself, life lost from wounds and sinking into the greedy embrace of senseless soil.

But it was just the bog, and a moon tinged from a duststorm, and five silhouettes staring at a small island of dirt, surrounded by a brackish pool. And at the slender tree rising from that mound, straining for the moon above it. She thought she could see it growing taller before her eyes, but was she simply sinking into the mud and thus fooled by a shifting perspective? Several large-billed birds lazily glided around the Second Spear, then settled to the ground beside it, unperturbed by the weight of prophecy. They paid no heed as Yaletha dropped to her knees in the mud and wept.

Chapter 6: In The Rough

City-dwellers greatly underestimate how much work there is simply in surviving. Most of them, taken outside the city, can't tell clean water from tainted, and in a dry land, don't know where to find it anyway. Their suppers are brought to them; those responsible for preparing those suppers do so with the fruit of the labors of others. They are unaccustomed to sleeping under the stars, and do not bring blankets or shelter, nor know how to use them effectively to keep warm during a cold desert night. And there are a hundred other needs in a day that they never give a second thought.

Yaletha and her companions, though slaves, were no different. There was never a moment they weren't wishing they had something that was plentiful in the city. Food was sparse on the great pasturelands of thorn-bushes, but when Oyana spotted a small prairie-dog scurrying into a warren, she had no spear to throw, nor a knife with which to carve one. They were too swift to chase, especially for slaves with bare feet, who had to step carefully just to avoid thorns and stones. If they had caught one, how would they skin it without knives, or cook it without fire, or eat it without knowing which parts were safe to eat?

These struggles were enough to drive them to weariness and despair, and yet all their answers would provide is warmth and food. But these Haebinnor had more to haunt them than hunger. There were Oritheri trackers seeking them. To be sure, the value of six slaves was, to the Oritheri, scarcely worth spending a day in the scrublands. But the example of six runaway slaves hanging from nooses in the Court of the Well, that was worth a great deal more effort. The hounds would be behind them for days, at least. Perhaps longer, if the cloaked men had anything to say about it. Perhaps much longer.

As the sun made its merciless climb across the sky, these struggles to survive seemed great enough to drive from Yaletha's mind, and even those of her friends, grand questions of destiny and prophecy. At times someone might inquire where they were going, what was next for them. Even this topic died quickly on their parched lips, since all they could do is head towards water, and away from the men hunting them.

It had been three days. They were sore, hungry, cold, and wracked with aches and blisters, but they were starting to figure out how to survive. Ulgi had taken to carrying Kumza or Yaletha at times, and between, he'd broken rocks to make sharp-edged pieces of stone that Thargoz used to carve makeshift spears, which Oyana and Jemik could toss with fair accuracy to catch a meal now and then. By trial and error, Yaletha worked out how to skin and butcher these meager morsels of meat. Kumza had spent more time in the scrublands than the others, gathering those plants whose leaves, oils, and nuts could soothe blisters and mend wounds; in addition to these, she found a few berries they could eat, a source of both food and precious moisture. She also managed to scrabble together a meager fire in the twigs of the thorn-bushes, adequate for cooking, or to huddle around for warmth.

They were arrayed around such a fire in the shelter of an overhanging stone; no Oritheri pursuer had been spotted for hours, and they were discussing the possibility that they'd given up, when Jemik spoke of the one thing Yaletha hoped never to hear again. "Whether they follow or not, we must start searching for the aurochs herd." When he was met with tired, uncomprehending stares, he explained, as if to a child, "To see the Third Spear." Before the resulting groans could marshal themselves into objections, he protested, "Surely you realize we have to see the Third Spear, don't you? I was right about going to the bog, to see the Second Spear, and still you gainsay me?"

Before Yaletha could retort, or more likely, withdraw, Thargoz tried to intercede on her behalf. "We don't know where the Third Spear will be, and we don't know that it will even happen. The prophecy warns of false signs. Even with two Spears seen, the day may not yet have come."

"Which is why we must find out, to be sure," Jemik answered. He'd clearly been rehearsing this answer for some time; he glanced at Yaletha hopefully, though whether he longed for support or simply attention, only he knew. "That's why we went to the bog."

"How did we end up there, anyway?" asked Kumza, looking around suspiciously. "I thought we were simply fleeing, aimlessly, and then suddenly there we were."

"The hand of Fate must have guided us there," Jemik proclaimed triumphantly.

Oyana cleared her throat and seemed about to speak, then stopped herself. It seemed clear she was caught on the knife-edge of something she had wanted to say, but felt she could not; it took some prodding before she finally confessed. "Yaletha, I'm sorry. I... I steered us towards the bog as we were fleeing. I thought, we had to go *somewhere*, and it might as well be there. Then we'd know. Perhaps the First Spear was just a happenstance, or a false sign. I hoped to put you to some ease when there was nothing there, that's all." She shot a pointedly defiant stare at Jemik. "It wasn't the hand of Fate, it was just my foolishness. And it's foolish to go to the Third Spear now, even if we knew where to go."

"It might yet have been," Jemik insisted, shaking his head. "You might have been how Fate intervened. As it might again, to bring us to the Third Spear."

"If it will, then let it," Thargoz argued. "We need not take any special effort. We should pursue our own safety and freedom, and if the Third Spear should be seen as we go, then let it."

Everyone began to speak at once, but Oyana cut through their voices. "If any Oritheri still pursue us, they will certainly be seeking the Third Spear. By now, the Haebinnor who gather water in the bog will have seen the Second Spear. A fortnight ago I would have been sure they would keep the secret, and that any Oritheri who chanced to visit the bog would not recognize the import of the Second Spear." Others were nodding their heads. "But when the First Spear was seen, by Haebinnor alone, the moon had not even arisen before Oritheri learned of it, knew what it meant, and moved against Yaletha. They must know more than we dare to fear."

His voice cracking, Thargoz said, "I might have been wrong about them being Oritheri. I must be. If the Oritheri know of the prophecy, we have already failed."

"We can't take the risk," Oyana concluded, brushing aside the mystery. "If the Oritheri know, they will find us at the Third Spear, and we will be hanged as an example. If we avoid seeking it, we may yet live as runaway slaves. And," she held up her spear-tip towards Jemik to hold off his protest, "if Fate wishes to guide us, it will. Thargoz may be a fool about some things, but here he speaks wisdom. We may choose as we deem best, without giving heed to Fate's whims; for Fate, as you speak of it, will have already laid the path before us such that our choices will go where it chooses."

"Fine words from the woman who led us to the bog," Jemik said sourly. "But we should at least keep a wary eye out for the aurochs herd. If we chance upon it, and one of our spears can take down a small one, we will have meat aplenty, and hides for blankets and sandals, and bones for tools. If we see a sign while we hunt, well, then, we see one, yes?"

"And what if we do not?" The voice was surprisingly strong; for a moment, heads turned seeking its source. Yaletha stood, her dark hair shining in the light of the burning thorn-bush. "What then, Jemik?" she continued, staring at him as if in accusation. "Will you let this lie? Already all our lives have been rent asunder, and we may not survive the night, and still you try with every breath to push me into peril, to make of me some hero."

Very little seemed to touch Jemik, but at these words, and at the surprising ferocity Yaletha showed in speaking them, he was visibly wounded. "I believe in you more than you do yourself," he protested, though with only a hint of his usual fervor. "I want the day to come, but more, I want the hand to be yours. And I want to be beside you

26

every stride. You know how I feel about you," and though she shook her head, he continued, "and I want what is best for you. And I believe that this is it. If I am the only one here who sees the greatness in you, Yaletha, know that I will be there when you finally see it, and need me to stand with you."

Only Kumza heard the soft murmur from Thargoz, which clearly he meant for no ears but his own. "Like you were the night they came for her, and she needed to be saved." They were bitter words, full of frustration. Yaletha showed no favor to either Jemik or Thargoz, but Kumza knew that Thargoz always felt slighted, trapped in the shadow of Jemik's boldness. She wanted to embrace him, to encourage him, to soothe his hurt, but she knew he would not welcome her comforts.

Nor would Yaletha, though Kumza wanted nothing more than to put her at ease. So deep was her hurt, even before the First Spear pointed to her. Kumza could see it more than anyone, and it pained her. This is why she'd taken up the healing arts: seeing hurt in the eyes of others always visited the same to her, and only by salving another could she heal herself. Wounds of the body could be tended with herbs and bandages, but hurts in the heart were the more pernicious. And Yaletha had suffered so many of them that she hid inside them, trying to protect herself. It was why she rebuffed both Jemik and Thargoz, and even kept Kumza's whispers at a distance.

Even now, with Jemik practically declaring his intentions before the whole group, Yaletha was drawing her pain around her to keep his blundering, tactless affections away. "You care only about the idea that this will be a grand adventure and you will be part of it." An unkind assessment; even Yaletha must know that, in his thoughtless and clumsy way, Jemik's affections for her were sincere. But Kumza knew the words were meant to injure him and drive him away, and thus, didn't need to be true. "If you care about me, heed my wishes. I want no part of these affairs. I am nothing, a weak and frail slave of no ability beyond the butchering of beasts. The Haebinnor need one with a storm in her eyes and a steady hand on the spear, a voice that leads men and women to war, and eyes that see over the horizon. Someone like you, or Oyana. If they depend on me, they will perish unto the last child. Go on your adventure, and leave me here to die, or live, as chance may choose. You have my blessing to become the First Hand. It's nothing to do with me."

So rarely did Yaletha even speak, and all the more rare for her to speak with such conviction and anger, the others were struck silent. She stood a moment more, the firelight dancing in her grey-green eyes as if there were lightning striking behind them, then turned and stalked off to curl up alone, on the other side of the outcropping.

Still there was silence. When it seemed Jemik was about to say something, probably something clumsy that purported to be an apology but wasn't, Kumza stood and prevented it by declaring, "It's been a long day, and the weariness in our feet comes out in our words. Let the sun of the morrow shine a new light on our questions and reveal new wisdom. Come, Ulgi, we need rest. Jemik, you seem unwearied; you may have first watch."

Oyana quirked an eyebrow; Kumza was not the type to give orders. Even when she guided Ulgi it was done gently, and because he needed her wisdom. Oyana watched Jemik, sensing how the torrent of words he'd been readying in answer to Yaletha's departure, was now jostling up against a confused answer to Kumza's unexpectedly sly command, making a muddle of his thoughts such that neither answer passed his lips. "Wise as ever, Kumza," she said, rising and moving to a sheltered spot of her own, which only further trapped Jemik.

By the time he'd cleared his thoughts enough, everyone had left the fire and found a place to rest. All that was left for him to do was to stalk around the camp-site disconsolately. "A day will come," he murmured to himself again and again, but those who heard wondered, was he referring to the prophecy, or some other longed-for event?

Chapter 7: The Slumbering Lynx

The fire died out as quickly as had the argument, and over the following days, they never rekindled it. Aimless, they wandered the vast scrublands, which provided just enough for them to survive but little more. They saw herds of horses, and occasionally small gatherings of aurochs, but not the great herd, the thundering of whose hooves could be felt leagues away, if the legends were true. Still, wherever they wandered, Jemik kept his eyes open. He would crouch, when no one else was looking, to examine and count hoof-prints in the ground.

She did not show it, but Oyana also watched for the signs and listened for the rumbling. Usually when Jemik was studying the footprints in what he took to be secrecy, Oyana was watching him do it, and studying his reaction. She was torn. There was a thrill in her blood that told her the day *had* come, and it whispered to her of duty to her people; she yearned to rise up, to fight, to see her people at last be freed. The prophecy's warnings, which she'd whispered to herself a thousand times, rang hollow. *If the sand-mouse awakens the lynx, or hurls the spear too soon, the blood spilled shall not be Oritheri.* She did not feel like being a sand-mouse. But still, she saw the pain in Yaletha's eyes, the fear, and above all, the wish to be quiet. She knew that Yaletha wanted nothing more than to be a sand-mouse. Why had Fate not chosen Oyana to be the First Hand? She longed more than anything to take that burden off her friend's shoulders. Both to release Yaletha from that haunted look, and perhaps more so, because she yearned to clutch a spear in her fist and stand defiantly, scream a challenge to the Oritheri Baugcaun and see his works rent and scattered.

The moon, now free of its crimson taint, rose and sank and rose again. Each sunrise greeted a First Hand, and her friends, more thin, cold, hungry, and weary than the last had seen. Under the merciless glare of the unshadowed noon sun, hours could pass without a thought of Spears, of Fate, of the First Hand; it was enough to seek water. They hadn't seen any Oritheri hounds, and indeed, few people at all. The occasional group of hunters, or

Haebinnor gathering horses to tame, or a caravan of horse-drawn wains making way from one city to another, perhaps heading for Lithgweth in the north; but more often, they were alone.

Even amongst themselves. They marched surrounded by friends, yet their disagreements, rivalries, and unhappiness kept them separated. With one exception.

Back in the city, Kumza and Ulgi had been forced to keep their feelings for one another quiet. It was an odd custom: the Oritheri allowed, even encouraged, the Haebinnor to pair up (after all, there wouldn't be any more to serve if they didn't). Yet they also had to be reminded that they did not choose their own fate. If a couple was reasonably discreet, drawing no attention (particularly amongst the Oritheri) to their choice of mate, even though everyone knew what was occurring, the Oritheri would pointedly look the other way. But once they made the mistake of proclaiming their marriage, the Oritheri felt obligated to separate them, a gesture against the defiance. Kumza and Ulgi has chosen each other several years ago, and it had long become a custom of habit, to keep the smallest of affections secret. It took several days before, realizing as runaways they no longer needed to maintain the pretext, they broke the habit; and once they did, they were practically inseparable, holding hands constantly and reveling in the freedom to lie together without concern for who might see.

Which only made the others feel all the more alone. Yaletha kept to herself and turned away from any who tried to speak to her; the weight of their expectations of her was wrapped around her like armor of stone, and while she was increasingly miserable in her isolation, she was only more so when anyone tried to reach out to her. Jemik and Thargoz spat at one another over any pretext, both because of their disagreement about how they should proceed, and their rivalry for Yaletha's entirely-absent affections. Trying to keep the group together required Oyana to remain at some distance from these disagreements and hurts, lest she become entangled in them, which was itself an isolation as wide as the sky.

30

And thus, Jemik was able to guide their path by the simple expedient of having no opposition. He would merely drift in one direction, and the others would eventually veer to follow, because both alternatives – getting too far apart, or re-opening the discussion of where to go – were unacceptable. He grew more eager as the signs of the great herd seemed more pronounced, and Oyana became more anxious about what she saw him seeing. Though bone-weary, she struggled to remain vigilant, to balance Jemik's boyish excitement.

It had been a fortnight since the First Spear, and Jemik was suddenly hurrying, under the light of the setting sun, to the top of a crest. Oyana could hear a faint, low sound: the rumbling of the aurochs herd, a sandstorm, or the beating of her own heart? Rather than rushing behind Jemik, she swept the horizons for danger, and was thus the first to see a dozen men and women approaching from the left, unnoticed by Jemik.

Crouching, she peered at them, holding her breath with anxiety. Then she released it. Rather than seeing the sallow skin and angular features of the Oritheri, what she saw under the ruddy sun was the olive of her own people. She hefted her makeshift spear and waved it, and soon the strangers, and her own company, were closing with one another, shouting greetings into the greedy wind, which carried them over the ridge. Jemik alone continued heedlessly on his course, perhaps too excited at the prospect of a vast aurochs herd, or perhaps simply unaware of the chance meeting.

"What brings so many so far?" Thargoz called as they finally were near enough to hear one another. Oyana frowned, thinking this an unnecessarily suspicious question. A fair one, but not setting the right tone. At least she thought so until she noticed how many of the dozen had their eyes on Yaletha. And not with the awe that might attend the knowledge that she was, at least if the signs were true, the First Hand; rather, they seemed suspicious. She moved closer to Yaletha and remained watchful and silent.

31

A slender and tall Haebinnor, almost as slight as Yaletha herself, stepped forward to speak for the group. "Moktig," he said with a bow, which led Thargoz to introduce himself in turn. "I might ask the same," Moktig went on, "but we seek the same thing." One hand gestured toward the ridge, up which Jemik still scrambled. "But for different cause. We must entreat you, turn back."

"We did not choose to be runaways, but nevertheless, we are," Thargoz answered. "We cannot go back."

"Then go another way, if you must go any way," Moktig answered. While his fellows were staying behind him, there was a cohesiveness to them that Oyana at once feared and envied. They were here for a singular purpose and prepared to act decisively in its pursuit, something her rag-tag fellowship could not claim. "We know what you believe. We have seen the signs. I myself gazed upon the tree in the bog, before it was torn down. But we do not believe it is time. You risk all of our people, without our consent. Sand in our breath. We ask you to turn away from this reckless path."

Oyana was silently grateful that Jemik was too far to hear; he would rail against this claim in the most impolitic way imaginable. But even Thargoz proved surprisingly defiant. "You saw the First Spear, and the Second Spear, and still you doubt?"

"A happenstance of lines, easily falsified. And a sapling not even a season old. There were indications," Moktig continued in almost a whisper, "that the sapling had grown elsewhere and been carried to the bog and planted there, perhaps but a day or two before the First Spear was seen."

"Do you dare accuse us of such deception?" Thargoz called out. Yaletha flinched at the intensity in his tone, though she seemed almost more hopeful than she had in days. "To what end?"

Moktig raised his hands in a gesture of pacification. "We only suspect that the signs are false. Whether that be by the hand of another, or by that of Fate itself, they are a temptation we must not follow. A temptation *you* must not follow." His eyes were fixed on Yaletha now. "The lynx yet slumbers. We must not awaken it."

Oyana knew that Thargoz was remembering axes in the dark. In a moment he would protest that the lynx was already awake. She wasn't sure what to think of this; it meant their efforts were doomed, if it were true, and how could it not be? But she was sure it would ill behoove them to say this before Moktig. She spoke quickly, before Thargoz could. "Peace, friends. We take no steps to awaken anyone, lynx or otherwise. It was not by our hands that the First Spear was seen, nor fashioned. Nor did we choose to escape; we were hounded hence. We saw the Second Spear, and we may yet see the truth or falsehood of the Third Spear," her eyes flashed to Jemik and back in an instant, "but we take no actions. The First Hand," she watched as Yaletha bristled at this title, "will act only if we are sure that it is time. Sand in their breath. We have spoken the words of warning to ourselves under an empty sky as oft as have you."

There was a low murmuring, and then a silence as the two groups stared each other down. Though he stayed at the rear, sheltering Kumza, Ulgi drew himself to his full height, and some of Moktig's men turned their gaze up, then took a step back. But still they stood, separated only by the hasty wind.

Then Moktig shook his head. "That may be, but we cannot take that risk." He gestured, and as the men and women behind him started to advance, fists raised, Oyana shook her head. Had it come to this? Haebinnor fighting with other Haebinnor?

The others had no weapons amongst them, while Oyana and Thargoz both had crude spears. But there were many more of them. "Thargoz, keep Yaletha safe any way you must," Oyana said, but as she stepped in front of the two of them, she caught Moktig's eye by raising her spear. And then dropped it to the ground behind her. "We shed no Haebinnor blood this day. But neither do we allow ours to be spilled."

It must have seemed a gesture of such bravado that even Moktig paused a moment. But Oyana's true intent was simply to buy time for Ulgi to arrive by her side. The great brute could, by himself, knock aside a half-dozen men before he was felled, in an honest donnybrook. Oyana was herself the match of any of her rivals, and she was sure Thargoz would find similar strength in himself if Yaletha were threatened. Out of the corner of one eye, she saw Jemik, standing atop the ridge, turning to wave to them. By now, he'd seen the aurochs herd, for Oyana was sure that it must be there, and that Moktig and his fellows had been circling it to watch for them. And any moment, Jemik would notice what was happening and come to their aid, she hoped, or perhaps feared.

The fighting was over before Jemik made it back down the ridge, though. Ulgi had only to toss two of them through the air like sacks of peas, and pound another to the ground, before some started to break off and retreat. There were many bruises earned on both sides, and Oyana thought she heard a shoulder popping out of place; but as she crouched and gasped for breath, wincing at a deep ache in her side, watching Moktig's unconscious form being carried away, she pondered how much worse things might have gone.

"The Oritheri warriors, clad in armor and carrying spears, axes, and bows, would have felled us in seconds," she murmured. "They would not run, even from Ulgi, even without their spears; they are the first to enter and the last to leave any battle, even a hopeless one. How, even with the First Hand and the Six Spears, can we ever hope to rise against them, with bare fists and feet, so quick to flee a fight?" She gathered up her makeshift spear and leaned heavily on it as Kumza moved amongst their number, assessing minor injuries and lecturing all and sundry on the perils of battle. "And what if Moktig is right? The lynx already is awake. Sand in their breath, sand in our breath."

34

Chapter 8: The Third Spear

While he'd been able to see the fighting, Jemik didn't get his knuckles bruised. From his vantage point, high on a ridge with the great aurochs herd behind him, so full of the promise of Fate, the fight seemed inconsequential, a mere interruption in the tale, over quickly. A few lunges, some kicks and punches, a few people flying through the air, and Ulgi standing over them like a tree studying the dust, and then it was done. And yet with the fight concluded and history itself beckoning just beyond the ridge, there they stood, gasping for air, Oyana rambling on about being awake or something similarly inconsequential.

He wanted to hurry them, quick as the wind, over the ridge. Somehow he was sure that once they saw the vast, majestic sprawl of the herd, thousands of mighty beasts to the horizon moving as one, they would be as swept up as he was in the certainty that the day had come, and that it was time to act. It hadn't occurred to him to wonder what action there was to take; he was simply swept, like a branch down a fierce river, by the need to act. And baffled about why the others, like stones unperturbed by that river, didn't feel the current.

While they were catching their breath and nursing their wounds, he stood and spun in place, gazing, searching. There. That hilltop with a single tree on it, overlooking the vast bowl of the plains beyond, that must be the place. *The crest of the sky.* "Hurry! I'm telling you, I saw it, the lone beast of white!" It was all he could do not to run off and leave them behind.

"What are you talking about?" Thargoz demanded sourly. He'd only traded a few blows with one of Moktig's men, before Ulgi had swept the man away, but he still had a black eye and a deep bruise on one leg, and was in no mood for Jemik's earnest but vapid enthusiasm.

"The lone beast! There," Jemik pointed over the ridge, "is the aurochs herd. *A throng of thunder dark as a shadow and wide as a sea,*" he recited. "And in it, near this side in fact, one aurochs with shaggy white fur. White."

"Did you see a spear marking on it?" Kumza asked, eliciting a scowl from Yaletha.

"I couldn't get near. You know how aurochs are."

"Yaletha could get close enough. She handles beasts every day for her master. She knows their ways like no one else," Kumza answered, deepening the scowl.

"And the crest of the sky?" Thargoz asked. It was clear he wanted to find a flaw in Jemik's thinking, but prophecy was so full of metaphor and vagueness, and with unexpected ways it might come to pass, that it was hard to argue with something as pronounced as one white-furred aurochs amongst a herd. They were, after all, strikingly rare.

Jemik pointed to the lone tree in the distance. "There's a sharp drop beyond that. Not so sharp that the aurochs will refuse to run over it, but sharp enough that, if you stood there, the land would be open below you, a vast bowl of emptiness. All you'd see is the sky."

He could tell that Thargoz thought this interpretation was a stretch, which itself made Jemik's blood boil. It was certainly no harder to believe than a tree rising from a bog, or patterns in hide. The Haebinnor had mused for generations about what the Third Spear might mean. *In a throng of thunder dark as a shadow and wide as a sea, a lone beast of white, marked with the Third Spear, shall be swept to the crest of the sky.* Many had concluded the throng must be the aurochs herd, but there was less agreement about the crest of the sky. But if the white-furred aurochs had a spear marking, and it was swept to this crest, surely that would match the sign, even Thargoz must see this!

"We might as well go watch," Oyana said, glancing at Yaletha sympathetically. "We've come all this way. And then we'll know." Finally, someone who could see what was plain before them. Jemik led them to the crest of the ridge, wishing they'd hasten their steps.

Of their company, only Yaletha had seen this herd before. The vista was breathtaking; thousands, perhaps tens of thousands, of vast creatures, each a mound of thick fur taller than Ulgi at the shoulders, all running as quick as the wind, moving together as if led by one hand. Nothing could stand before such a throng. And they were, indeed, heading in the direction of the crest Jemik had pointed out.

Most startlingly, there, near the left flank of the herd, was a single white-furred aurochs. While there'd been aurochs with a white hide from time to time, even Yaletha had never seen one with her own eyes before. But did it bear the mark of a spear? Jemik was sure it must, but he could tell the others were less so. He was marshaling some arguments that Yaletha could run out amongst the beasts and see it with her own eyes, when he was brought up short as he spied the same thing the others were exclaiming about.

Archers. Dozens of Oritheri archers on horseback, racing alongside the herd, trying to catch up with the white-furred aurochs. Even Jemik could immediately divine their intent. If the aurochs died here, it could not fulfill the prophecy, and the Third Spear would be seen by the Haebinnor as a false sign. By, for instance, Moktig and his fellows, who were recovering from the brawl not a quarter-league away, well within sight of the crest.

"They went to such pains to be sure that the First Spear be proved false without revealing their knowledge of the prophecy to any but us, who were marked for death," Thargoz was musing, "and here they ride in the open, in full sight of a dozen Haebinnor."

"Perhaps those, too, are marked for death," Oyana answered.

Why were they worrying so much about this? The time for action was plainly arrived. "We have to stop them!" he cried out, waving his arms. "We have to save the lone beast of white."

"How?" Oyana answered, whirling on him with an accusing glare faster even than Thargoz could. "You're uninjured and unwearied. Perhaps you can single-handedly defeat a dozen mounted archers in full armor."

There was a moment when Jemik thought she meant it, and he was considering how to go about it, before he realized she'd been sarcastic. He frowned and fell to thinking, trying to come up with a plan. The thundering of the herd grew louder, filling the silence as it stretched on. The archers would be in range soon. And still he had no ideas.

"I can save the white one, but I'd need a horse, and for the archers to be busy for a few moments."

Jemik looked around, unsure at first who'd said this. He found everyone staring at Yaletha, who was standing with her shoulders slumped as if she hoped to sink into the ground and vanish.

Another pregnant moment passed before Jemik asked her, "How?"

"I've ridden amongst the herds before, to separate out the one that my master wishes, many times. I know the flow of the beasts, and how to calm the horse enough to slip into that flow. I can guide the white aurochs..." Here Jemik was about to object at the idea of bringing it closer to the edge of the herd where it would be more vulnerable, but before he could, Yaletha continued, "Guide it farther into the center of the herd. Out of bowshot, at least long enough for it to reach the crest."

"You shouldn't have to!" Kumza objected with uncharacteristic fervor. "The prophecy should provide for itself."

"And so it would, if they," Jemik stabbed a finger in the direction of the horsemen, "weren't interfering to prevent it."

"Even so," Kumza argued, but with far less certainty.

"But I would need…" Yaletha was trying to continue as if Kumza had not raised an objection, but her determination was flagging. "You would have to engage the archers. Knock one off its horse, and keep the others so focused on you that they couldn't fire at me until I was deep enough into the herd."

Another few moments passed while her fellows thought this through and reached the conclusion that Jemik alone spoke aloud, unnecessarily: "We will be captured or killed." But after a moment, he shrugged off the gloom of this assessment. "But the prophecy will go on. The First Hand will lead our people to freedom." He whirled around and stared at the archers. "That one. I'll run there, past those rocks, and come out in front of them. Oyana, Thargoz, throw your spears at the two on either side. You don't have to hit them, just make them swerve, and I can leap up and knock the one with the red helm crest off his horse. Then she can take the horse in the chaos, and the rest will have to rear up to get around us and the rocks, and that will buy some time. We can make it more by running into the way."

And he was already running down the ridge. "That is if they don't just put a dozen arrows in you before you even reach the rocks," Oyana called out bitterly at his back, but she was following him, unsure of why. And Thargoz, spear in hand, and then Ulgi with Kumza on his shoulders.

Even though she'd had a hand in it, Yaletha was bewildered by the audacity of this plan. Jemik paused and called out to her, "Hurry!" He could see the hesitation plain on her face. "No one else but you could do this. This is what I said, this is why Fate chose you! You are the First Hand!" She scowled, but she started down the hill, her fleet footsteps easily making up the distance. Perhaps simply drawn along by the momentum of the rest of the fellowship, Jemik wondered.

The plan had seemed like madness, but for once, Jemik had the right of it. The Oritheri did not expect to be opposed at all, and certainly not by something as daring as an attack by barefoot slaves. The crude spears would likely have glanced off of their armor, but in the split second that an unexpected spear is flying at a man, he doesn't calculate such things, he swerves. Jemik was lying on the ground in a tangle of limbs with one Oritheri warrior, while Yaletha was whispering to his horse, and then with a leap she was on its back and charging into the herd before the steed had even come to a stop. There was a baffling swirl of spooked horses and confused Oritheri, pinned between boulders. One man in maille was suddenly flying through the air over Jemik, while Ulgi was crying out from the pain of his fist making contact with the man's armor so effectively.

Jemik hauled himself to his feet. He had a few moments before his opponent could pull his armor-clad body up, during which he watched Yaletha, sliding through the herd like a leaf carried on a breeze. Already she was within a stone's throw of the white aurochs, and more, the herd was shifting around her, nudged by her slightest movements, the current carrying some towards the center and others away from it.

It would take her a few minutes to drive the white beast out of bow range. Jemik turned to face the man he'd unhorsed. Already, the other Oritheri were rallying, forming a circle around him and his companions. Arrows were nocked and pointed. Even he could imagine no way to escape from this.

40

But while they were capturing the five of them, they weren't firing at Yaletha, nor the white-furred beast. They may not even have realized she was present yet, let alone what she was doing. Jemik raised his fists and bellowed a challenge. If he made this capture difficult, it would take longer, and buy her more time. He saw Oyana following his lead, and soon, Ulgi as well, though the large man might have intended an actual fight rather than a stalling tactic. No matter, it would work either way, and Kumza would quiet Ulgi when it was time to surrender.

It was a few moments before it occurred to him that Thargoz was nowhere to be seen. He fumed. The coward! The day had come to stand, to fight. To defend Yaletha, and the Haebinnor. And Thargoz always hung about Yaletha, hoping to win her hand. Now he'd shown his true colors. He had fled, while Jemik remained steadfast. Now, surely she would finally see that Jemik was her true match.

That is, if any of them survived. He threw his hands up in a gesture of surrender, but he turned to watch the herd cresting the hill. Half of the Oritheri were still racing alongside, but none could reach the white aurochs, so deep inside the herd. There! The white aurochs was reaching the crest! *In a throng of thunder dark as a shadow and wide as a sea, a lone beast of white, marked with the Third Spear, shall be swept to the crest of the sky.* He could feel the flow of Fate as if it were the wind itself. Surely there would be no more arguing now about whether the day had come.

There were no more grave injuries by the time the Oritheri were leading them across the plains, their hands and feet bound in great chains. In the distance there was some kind of wain, a great covered cart pulled by four horses; it was clearly where they were being led. Somehow, being brought in chains didn't dampen Jemik's spirits. He knew he was being marched to his death, but all was well in the world. The day had come, and he'd helped to keep Fate on course

At least until he was close enough to the wain to see that one prisoner had reached it before them. There, surrounded by four Oritheri, was Yaletha, in chains.

There was a steely look in her eye as the five of them were being loaded into the wain. Jemik had never seen it before, and he had no idea what to make of it.

Chapter 9: An Uncertain Fate

If there was to be any elation at saving the white-furred aurochs, seeing the Third Spear, having a hand in making it happen, it was short-lived. Even Jemik slumped as he was manhandled onto the back of the wain, and did not put up a fight as his captor – the red-crested helm made it plain it was the man he'd unhorsed, though now that he had a chance to notice, he realized it was actually a woman – affixed the chain between his manacled wrists to a hook in the wain's floor.

It creaked as it started to roll, slowly at first, across the plains. As it picked up speed, the jostling reminded them all of their aches and bruises. By now even Kumza had suffered a few. There was a chorus of groans, and soon, silence, as they pondered their uncertain fate.

It was Oyana who started to speak at last, quietly enough that their captors, riding up front, might not overhear. "How did you get captured?" she asked Yaletha.

"Well, I could hardly ride forever, alone, in the plains," she answered bitterly. "Particularly with a half-dozen archers watching me. I had to leave the herd. The horse wouldn't go over the crest. I would have been trampled if I hadn't guided her out, and worse yet, the horse would have been, too. The archers were waiting for me."

"But the white aurochs? It was swept to the crest?" Jemik asked, weary but still hopeful.

"It was," Yaletha answered. "And yes, it had a marking like a spear, down its left flank. Brown, and hazy, but definitely a line and point. The hide was shockingly white, and seemed unhealthy. Ragged, like it was falling out in patches. I hope the poor thing is well." She had, only a few weeks earlier, helped her master and his hunters kill several, and had butchered them herself; yet the thought of one falling to illness, rather than a swift end from a well-placed arrow, troubled her.

"Then the prophecy holds," Jemik proclaimed.

"Even if it does," Yaletha protested, "what good is it? The First Hand is now in the very claws of the lynx, a lynx long since awake. They've known about the prophecy all along, and they've been carefully ensuring that no one realized that they know. How can you think this can end well? The coming of the signs now is our death knell, not a sign of our rebellion. The lynx is awake, and all the sand-mouse has for a First Hand is me, and here I am, in chains."

Even Jemik couldn't muster enough determination to try to argue with her. They were silent for a time. Yaletha peered out through a gap in the timbers of the wain. Some while later, she whispered, "Lithgweth."

"What?" asked Ulgi. At Kumza's urging, he'd given up testing the chains. Even his strength was no match for well-forged iron.

"Where they're taking us. The city of the Oritheri Baugcaun. Why to the capital, I wonder? It's a day's ride even in a wain."

"The Fourth Spear," Jemik said breathlessly, but no one answered his observation.

They were silent a time longer. Yaletha wondered to herself, and finally, she asked. "What came of Thargoz?" She'd been afraid the answer might be, as seemed most likely to her, that his body was cooling, arrows rising from it, near the boulders.

"Coward," Jemik spat. "He abandoned us. Betrayed us. Showed his true colors at last."

"Don't be absurd," Oyana protested. "Why would he have saved Yaletha from those axe-men back in the city if he were a traitor?"

"Perhaps he's the one who led them there," Jemik answered. "Told them about the prophecy."

"Then why fight them?" Yaletha asked, wanting desperately to dismiss Jemik's thoughts.

"Maybe he wanted to impress you," Jemik answered. "Or he hadn't expected them to go so far."

Oyana tugged pointless at her chains. "But why would he? What's his reason to do any of this?"

Jemik was at a loss to answer that. It was, surprisingly, Ulgi who offered an answer, though not intending to. "Why Moktig did? Why any of ours do?" While it seemed beyond reason for any of them, they had just seen a demonstration how some of their own people might stand against them. How they might feel more comfortable in the chains they knew, than to take the ultimate risk. And Thargoz had a kind mistress. He was given furs to sleep on, and rarely was punished despite being more defiant than most. Perhaps he'd preferred that life to the danger.

Kumza also found herself wondering if he might not have chosen to sabotage their efforts to protect Yaletha. He'd seen how much it pained her to be the First Hand, and he knew that the First Hand would be in grave danger. While she found she could, surprisingly, believe he might betray them, if he thought he was doing the right thing by doing it, she could not believe he was anything but deeply in love with Yaletha. His eyes told a tale that could be naught but true. And love can, especially in perilous times, drive a man to acts he would never believe himself capable of. If so, the poor fool would be regretting his actions now. Kumza felt sorry for him. Even as she was carried in chains to her execution, she could still feel sorry for the man who'd helped put her there.

Those chains couldn't keep Jemik's spirits down long. "Even so, Fate will not be so easily stymied. We've seen three of the Spears, you cannot deny it any longer. The day has come. Somehow, we will triumph yet."

Before Yaletha could repeat her protest, Oyana asked. "How then can the First Hand be freed from this trap, to go on and cast to the clouds the Sixth Spear?"

They were silent a few moments. Then Oyana began to murmur the first words of the prophecy, hoping that it would clear her mind, or suggest something. "*A day will come...*" But she fell silent almost immediately, for at once, in harmony with her, a haunting, low, deep voice was speaking the same words. She stared raptly at Ulgi, astonished at his mellifluous recitation. The man usually couldn't form a proper sentence, but of course, Oyana realized, he knew these words, as all the Haebinnor did; and when he spoke them, his voice was like the sighing of the earth itself.

A day will come, foretold by signs six in number, when the Spears of the Haebinnor shall challenge the sky, and on that day shall the fates of the Haebinnor and Oritheri be known. Not the wisest amongst the East or West may know how true the spear shall fly until it is cast. If it fly true, the Oritheri shall perish, their works rent by the sky until not one grain stands atop another, and none shall mourn them while the Haebinnor walk free beneath the stars. But take heed! False signs shall be seen; only when all six unfold shall the day be right. If the sand-mouse awakens the lynx, or hurls the spear too soon, the blood spilled shall not be Oritheri.

The First Hand shall fell, trembling, a beast of noble blood, within whose very flesh will be scribed a spear circled; and thus shall the First Spear be seen, and the First Hand known. From mud clinging shall grow the living Second Spear, straining for the bleeding moon. In a throng of thunder dark as a shadow and wide as a sea, a lone beast of white, marked with the Third Spear, shall be swept to the crest of the sky. The Fourth Spear shall fly, cast by a mighty bow, to shatter glass and set loose a flock of white birds across the sky of Lithgweth. The sky itself shall cast the Fifth Spear to rend asunder the Oritheri Rhîs unto shattered stones. And at the last, the First Hand shall cry defiance to the sky itself, casting to the clouds the Sixth Spear from atop the Spire of Last Days.

This day shall come; no storm, no hand, no will, and no axe may stop it. The spear shall drink blood without heed to whose blood it is, and a people shall fall. Until that day, the Haebinnor must remain quiet as sand-mice, and let no word of these hopes reach the ears of the Oritheri, that they may revel in luxuries and be slumbering when the spear is cast. But if the people be unruly or riotous, the lynx shall devour the sand-mice, and the Haebinnor shall fall, sand in their breath, and perish unto the last child, to the end of days.

The others whispered the words, or simply mouthed them, in time. No Haebinnor could resist their call. Yet in the echoes of Ulgi's voice, they murmured without voice, and when the last word slipped into the air and faded, there was a long, reverent moment of silence.

"If it shall come to pass," Yaletha said at last, "there must be another First Hand. For soon, we shall be put to the axe." She was still peering through the slats. "Behold. Lithgweth."

Chapter 10: Lithgweth

The first impression one gets on seeing the city of Lithgweth is that it seems bland and monochromatic. Every building, every street, every wall, every tower is fashioned of the same color of stone. So uniform that the eyes play tricks; walls and floors merge, and everything blurs into a confusing jumble of shadows and perspective. Making matters worse, the streets are perfectly straight, evenly spaced, and arrayed in a logical and efficient fashion that only makes it all the easier for the uniformity to twist vantage points in on themselves. In most cities, to find your way around, you ignore the people, the wains, the horses, the dangling laundry, and the thousand other oddments of city life, and focus on the buildings and streets; but here, you have to do the opposite, using the location of these objects to orient yourself and identify how shadows reveal walls or archways, turns and joinings.

From within the wain, peering out through gaps in the slats, the Haebinnor had little opportunity to see this. Instead, they could only stare at a thin slice of a wall as it rolled past, the wain creaking its way through the streets at a surprisingly brisk pace. The first thing that Oyana noticed was that the route was circuitous and winding, and as she watched more closely, it was clear why. Virtually every person they passed was Oritheri. She knew there were many Haebinnor in service here, but the wain-driver was choosing a path that avoided the places they were likely to be, for reasons she could only puzzle over.

Kumza's eyes focused on something else. "The walls," she whispered, awestruck. "They're sand."

"What of it?" Yaletha asked sourly.

"No, not sandstone… Sand. It's… it's moving."

It was Jemik who answered, his native excitement rising up. "I've heard stories of this!" he exclaimed. "The Crimson Sorcerers built the city anew. Do you recall the tale?" Oyana was growing more and more impatient with Jemik, but he didn't wait long enough for her to try to stop him, and it wouldn't've worked anyway. "The old city was on the hilltop north of here, but it was destroyed, almost utterly, in a sandstorm that lasted ten days and ten nights. All that remains is one ruined tower, the Spire of Last Days."

"Yes, we all know that," Yaletha barked. "That is where I was supposed to cast the Sixth Spear to the clouds, whatever that means."

"The king at the time, this is before they were called Oritheri Baugcaun, he escaped, but only barely. The queen, the Oritheri Rhîs, wasn't as lucky. They say the sands flayed her flesh from her bones in an instant while she still lived. So the king, he called his advisor…"

"The Oritheri Cowr," Kumza said. Apparently she was listening raptly, though she was still staring out the gap in the wain's boards.

"Yes, though again, that title wasn't used yet," Jemik answered. "He was called, and charged to find a means that a city could be built, which could never be torn down by a sandstorm again, at any cost. He spent years seeking wisdom from the farthest lands, and at the last, they say he struck a bargain with the Crimson Sorcerers. Scores of sorcerers toiled for years to craft a spell that captured a sandstorm itself within a crystal, the very crystal that sits atop the Oritheri Baugcaun's scepter to this day, they say."

"And thus, the Oritheri Baugcaun can use his pet sandstorm to fight off another that threatens his city?" Oyana asked, thinking it unwise to encourage Jemik in spinning his tall tale, but also thinking she might bring him to the point, and thus, the conclusion sooner.

"No!" Jemik answered, loud enough to earn a barked order to hush from the wain-driver. "The sandstorm was captured, but only its heart, the spirit of the sandstorm itself, is in the stone. As mountains and rivers have spirits dwelling in them, so too, sandstorms. And this storm's spirit is trapped in the scepter. The Oritheri Baugcaun holds the scepter and its sorcery, and controls the spirit, and through her, the sandstorm, forcing it to shape its winds as walls

50

and towers and streets. The entire city, it *is* the sandstorm. The sand in the walls is always moving because the walls are simply the winds, holding the sand in place. And from this is fashioned towers and palaces and granaries and streets, and even the aviary."

"I've never heard something so absurd in my life," Oyana protested, "and I've known you for most of it, so that's saying a lot."

"And yet," Kumza said, "if you look, you can see the sand in the walls is swirling, just as sand in a storm, though the wall itself is solid as stone. Stranger tales have been told, of sorcerous powers in the lost ages of the past."

Before Oyana could lodge another protest, or even decide if she might believe this far-fetched tale, Jemik called out eagerly once more. "Look, the aviary! The Fourth Spear!"

"It's never been agreed for certain that the aviary is what the Fourth Spear speaks of," Oyana answered wearily.

"But it must be," Jemik protested. *"The Fourth Spear shall fly, cast by a mighty bow, to shatter glass and set loose a flock of white birds across the sky of Lithgweth.* The only white birds in the city are the doves that had been kept as pets by that very queen who perished. She had left orders they, and all their get, be tended. The few that survived kept returning to the site of their long-lost cote, so the king included an aviary when this city was shaped, and those doves, and their young, and their young, have been kept there ever since, in memory of the lost Oritheri Rhîs. They are kept in with glass windows that might be broken with a well-placed bowshot. Where else could you find white birds freed by glass?"

While Oyana could hardly argue with that, she wanted to. She ached to rail at Jemik, to reach over somehow, even if meant breaking the chains to do it, and physically vent her frustration on his body. Why even worry about the Fourth Spear? The Oritheri knew, had long known, of the prophecy. The First Hand was chained and being brought to an uncertain but clearly unfavorable fate, probably her death. Hope had fled, sand in its breath. And still he rambled like a child telling bedtime stories about things too grand to be believed. Someone should shut his mouth with a closed fist, and she wished, at that moment, it could be her.

She was still choosing her words, hoping to be just acerbic enough to silence him, but not so much as to elicit another round of his grating voice, when the wain suddenly tilted onto two wheels and nearly toppled over.

From within the wain they had no idea what was happening. Ulgi was hanging almost suspended in the air as the wain yawed, his considerable weight held by the chains on his wrists and ankles. Jemik was thrown bodily into Yaletha, whose elbow was now lodged in Oyana's gut. Kumza still had her eye to the gap in the boards when they veered towards the ground; she was shrieking. It seemed for sure the wain would grind itself to pieces, and its occupants with it, as it wobbled and teetered at an untenable angle while still careening forward at a perilous pace. Outside there were screams and shrieks, some from people and some from horses.

52

The moment hung motionless and then, with a lurch, the wain righted itself. The wheels nearly cracked as it slammed back down and almost tilted over the other way. By now it was canted at an angle and nearly wedged between one wall and some sort of stall that stood in the street. They could hear more sounds of fighting as they slowly, achingly righted themselves. Although Ulgi had had the worst of the incident's trauma, due both to his size and the happenstance that he'd been on the side of the wain that had risen up, he was nevertheless testing the chains to see if they'd worked loose in the jostling, but it seemed they hadn't.

The sounds of struggle outside came to a stop only a few seconds later, punctuated by the sound of someone having the wind knocked out of him and crumpling to the ground. "Wait," an Oritheri voice barked. "Don't kill him. The Oritheri Cowr will want him with the others."

They waited silently in the wain for a few minutes until the back was opened, and then, in chains, bruised, bloodied, and clearly just barely conscious, Thargoz was dragged up into the wain by two of the Oritheri and affixed to one of the hooks.

No one knew what to say for a few moments. The wagon sat still while a few quick repairs were performed, and the six of them stared at one another. But mostly at Thargoz. No one wanted to be the one that asked what had happened. Not even Jemik, though his reasons might have been sharpest. At last, as the wain started to move again, Thargoz coughed and said, "Well, that didn't go as I'd hoped."

It was as if the pressure in Oyana suddenly burst. "What didn't? What in the name of the Six Spears is going on?"

"I tried to rescue you. I suppose I failed."

Jemik was shaking his head. "You? You're the one who betrayed us in the first place!"

Thargoz seemed baffled by this. "Betrayed? What?"

53

"When we were being captured, you fled, like a coward. You're probably the one who told the Oritheri where we were, and about the prophecy." Jemik was railing at Thargoz but his eyes were on Yaletha, who was looking away from both of them the best she could, trying to hide inside herself, trying to shut it all out.

"What? No, I saw that they were going to capture us. I thought we'd stand a better chance of getting free if one of us was already free, to rescue the others. I've been following the wain at a distance all along, but I couldn't even catch up, let alone overpower the six Oritheri warriors that have been walking with it. I kept in the shadows in the city and followed; no one notices a slave on his way somewhere, not even a tired and bruised one. When I saw where you were heading, towards the palace of the Oritheri Baugcaun..."

Oyana said in a dry, bitter voice, "Is that where we're heading?"

"Well, yes, it's..." Thargoz tried to turn around. "Oh, I see. You can't really see the city from here, you can't see the palace that's ahead. It can be naught else but that of the Oritheri Baugcaun."

"We can see a bit through the gaps," Kumza interjected.

"So I ran along streets that went parallel. Everything's all in straight lines. Did you notice the walls? They're made of..." Thargoz stopped at the wordless silencing stare from Oyana, and gulped. "Anyway, I got ahead of the wain, got up onto a roof, and pushed a keg down into the path so that the wain would have to stop. Only I didn't time it quite as well as I hoped, and the wain rolled up onto it. I was jumping down, planning to land on the roof and pull the door open. I thought if I could get Ulgi free, he could get us the rest of the way. But the wagon canted and I hit the roof while it was swinging. It tossed me into the wall, and then the Oritheri were on me." He sighed and added, "It wasn't a very good plan, even if the keg had fallen where I meant. But it was all I could think to do."

"It might have worked anyway, had Ulgi not been on that side," Oyana said. "The wain would have broken to pieces if it tipped over at that speed, but any of us who survived might have gotten free. But his weight brought it back down."

Jemik was fuming. He'd invested a lot in the idea that his rival was a traitor, and it was plain he was trying to think up some way that it might still be true, that this could be some complicated ruse. Before he could think of one, Yaletha asked, "Why even bother?"

This took Thargoz back a moment. He started to answer, stopped, started again. Finally, he said, his eyes on her, "Because I couldn't abandon you."

"Because I'm the First Hand?" she asked.

"No. I mean, maybe. I'm not even sure if I believe that. I'm not sure what to believe. But isn't it enough that it be because of who you are, and how I feel about you?" He added as an afterthought, "And about all of you. You're all my friends."

Jemik snorted. "How you feel about her? You weren't there. When they were beating us down, I was beside her. I was taking blows meant for her. And you were off somewhere hiding like a coward. You only changed your mind later because you thought you could win her back without even getting a bruise."

"Just because I didn't stand there getting pummeled doesn't mean I don't care," Thargoz spat. "What she needed was someone with their wits about them, someone who could help her when she needed help. What good did you do her, stuck in here with no chance of freeing her?"

"You mean, the same place you are?"

"At least I had a chance to get her free. You never did. You'd rather get beaten up and look like you're defending her, than actually defend her. Well, if that's what matters, I stood up to her attackers a fortnight ago, when you were nowhere to be seen, so I suppose we're even on that count."

"That is, if you weren't the one who brought them to her," Jemik exclaimed. "You—"

"Stop!" Yaletha's voice grated like sand across stone, and her eyes flashed like a storm brewing. "Both of you. It doesn't matter. We're all going to be dead before the sun sets. I don't want to spend my last day under the sun with the two of you trying to put me in between you. Now be quiet. I don't want to hear another word." Jemik and Thargoz both almost started to talk, but her eyes narrowed and they both bit back their words and averted their gaze.

There was nothing to keep them company the rest of the way to the palace other than the creaking of the wain, the aching of their bones, and the bitterness of their private thoughts.

Chapter 11: Truth and Lies

They could only wonder why they were being displayed for the Oritheri Baugcaun since he hardly seemed interested. They stood there in chains, with guards on all sides, and even had their ankle-chains pinned to the stone floor, while he paraded around them, looking at them and making tut-tut noises. Kumza couldn't keep her eyes off the scepter in his hand. A crystal sphere perched at its apex, in which swirled, endlessly, a handful of sand. Each grain was tossed in an unseen wind to career chaotically, heedless of the other grains; and yet somehow, every few heartbeats, as if by the most improbable turn of chance, these came together to make the shape of a tiny person trapped in the crystal, hands pressed against its inner surface. Just for a flicker, barely long enough for the eye to perceive; then the grains continued on their courses and all was chaos within once more, until the next such chance meeting.

For a warlord who had ruled over a tribe of conquerors for longer than Yaletha had been alive, the Oritheri Baugcaun seemed unassuming, easily overlooked. He wore only a robe, and for all that it glimmered with golden threads, it added little gravity to the man. He was hardly taller than her. His sallow skin was wrinkled and pocked, and he'd lost most of his hair, leaving only a few tufts of incongruous white. But in his eyes was a spark of authority, or of cruelty; she could imagine, if he were arrayed in shining armor and standing tall, with those eyes he might seem like a king, like a man that men would follow. Out of fear, not loyalty, but follow all the same.

Around them he walked, studying them, and then around again. He stopped before Yaletha. "This?" he asked, shaking his head. Behind him, the Oritheri Cowr stood, his expression lost in the shadows of a deep cowl. "She is scarcely a meal for one of my dogs. Are you sure?" The Oritheri Cowr nodded, but as the Oritheri Baugcaun was still staring into Yaletha's eyes, he couldn't've seen this answer. "Well, do as you deem best with them, then. Just be sure the rest are put back into their place, beneath our heels."

Then they were led off, chained one to the other, down yet more hallways. The sameness of the stone was still evident here, but bedecked with so much adornment, fine silks, rich brocade, furniture carved from wood from a hundred leagues away, trophies from battles in the north, and a thousand things besides, that the hue almost was lost amongst the decadence. As they moved farther from the Oritheri Baugcaun's chambers, the halls became more and more sparse, and soon they were winding up narrow stairs.

At last, they were brought into a surprisingly spacious chamber in a high tower. The room was sparsely furnished: a desk covered in books and scrolls, a huge bed piled high with white silk sheets, and a few personal effects. The only decoration was the impressive views commanded by the narrow windows, showing the entire city arrayed below. Pressed close to the wall and peering through the glass, Yaletha could see hundreds of homes and shops neatly arrayed in straight lines, warehouses and barracks, plazas and marketplaces, forges and stables; and girdling it all, fortified walls crested with ballistae and watch-towers. A glint of light far to the south made her wonder, was that the glass of the aviary?

Warriors were stationed around the circle of the room, a dozen at least. The six slaves stood to one side of the room, across from the desk, while the door was securely locked. "Now, then," the Oritheri Cowr purred in a voice like tainted honey, "we can dispense with these. You have much to see before the end." He moved from slave to slave, flanked by two warriors with spears at the ready, and removed their chains. Ulgi almost lunged at him once freed, despite the number of warriors that he could not hope to defeat, but Kumza stayed his hand with a whisper.

Before the vizier could say more, Thargoz asked, "How long have the Oritheri known of the Six Spears?" It seemed pointless to be coy about it now.

The Oritheri Cowr laughed. "Oh, my dear boy, this will be such delight. Do you know that I am the tenth to bear this title? When one of the Oritheri rise to a position so exalted as mine, we give up our old name, and are known by only the title thenceforth. In fact, I cannot even recall what my name was before. But I do know the name of the first of my title." He tapped one of the books on the desk. "Not that it matters to you. What matters is what he did. He was a most cunning man, which is from whence comes the title."

"I'm sure he knew how to tie his own shoes," Thargoz murmured dryly.

The Oritheri Cowr was undaunted and unbaited. "How long have we known of your prophecy, the secret of the Haebinnor? Why, my dear boy, we've known it longer than you have. And the reason for this is simple. We were the ones to invent it."

Amongst the stunned gasps that resulted, Oyana protested, "Invented it? Do you mean, foresaw it?"

A thin, sibilant voice like that belonging to the Oritheri Cowr is not the type suited to a booming laugh, but he made one anyway. It was a wheezing, pathetic sound, like breaking stones. "The first of my line foresaw only this: that a recently-conquered people would not accept their subjugation easily. But there is no more potent weapon than hope. He sat in this very room, at this very desk, and labored with his quill. Using words as his tools, he forged a chain out of the stuff of hope itself. He penned the words here, and then set his agents to whispering it into the ears of the Haebinnor."

"To what end?" Thargoz spat.

"In the generations since, there has never once been an uprising of your people," the Oritheri Cowr purred. "Now and then, there's a hint of one, but soon, your own people put it down for us, out of fear of sand in your breath. Even when one of your kind is merely a bit too defiant, too unruly, others will press him to accept his service, to meekly obey, to keep us lulled into our lynx's slumber. We hardly need to chain you or whip you. You do it to yourselves for us. You are the best slaves; you spare your masters even the work of enslaving you."

An hour before, Yaletha would have thought her spirits could sink no lower. The lynx was awake, her people had a hopelessly incapable First Hand heading to the gallows, and the Haebinnor were doubly doomed to perish utterly. But this was all the worse. There *never* had been true hope. Her people had been their own oppressors, and she had been amongst the worst of them.

"You're lying," Jemik proclaimed. "This is a trick to break our spirits. We've seen three of the Spears, *three* of them, just as the prophecy foretold."

The Oritheri Cowr frowned and tapped a finger to his lips. "And this is a puzzle. I had thought you were falsifying the signs yourself. It's happened before, several times. This is why we sent people to prevent you from doing so. But it became clear you were not, yourselves, responsible. You've been being played, and I would very much like to know by whom."

Jemik was having none of it. "Pretty words make pretty lies."

Whirling to face him, the Oritheri Cowr seemed about to strike, but stopped. "It amuses me to see what this knowledge does to you. Look, there, your mewling First Hand can barely stand up. If I bared my chest and placed a knife in her hand, would it find my heart, or her own? You do not know. But you," he prodded Jemik's chest with a clawed fingertip, "require more to break your feckless spirit. Tell me this. You have been reciting this prophecy under your breath every day of your life, but has anyone ever told you who was the one to foresee it?"

His mouth wide open to offer a challenging answer, Jemik was surprised to find no words in it. In fact, it had never occurred to him to wonder. As a child, like any of the Haebinnor, he was taught the words in secret by his parents, when he was too young to understand them. By the time he knew what they said, they'd become so familiar that the moment to wonder about their source had passed. It was enough to know they'd come to him from his parents, and their parents, and theirs.

A heavy, dusty book, so old it required care to lift lest its covers fall apart, was now being brought before him by the Oritheri Cowr. "See, here, on this page, my predecessor writes of his plan, and how it will be carried out." One bony finger almost stabbed at a page, but held back to avoid damaging the fragile parchment. "And here, the first draft of the prophecy. You can even see where he crossed out words and changed them, to make the signs more implausible, but not so implausible that your people could not hang on their possibility. Do you see?" When he noticed the look of blank incomprehension on Jemik's face, he stepped back. "Of course you do not. You have no letters. Which of you can read?"

Kumza hesitantly raised a hand, and the book was brought before her. She pondered it carefully. Another might have, out of spite, struck it, shattering it to dust, but Kumza was not the sort to think of this. And if she had, she would deplore the idea of destroying such a venerated artifact, even if it were one that damned her people. At last she whispered, "It is as he says."

"The pages are false," Jemik protested. "He's created it to fool us."

"They are old," Kumza said. "And the ink, by its hue, is made from the sap of a tree that once grew near here, but which withered when the hot winds from the southwest came. Yes, it's possible to bring in the ink, or sap, from Ahdnak," she added to forestall the objection she anticipated from Jemik, "but why would he bother? To use a rare, costly ink just to fool us, when it was unlikely any of us would know enough of herb-lore to recognize the ink anyway? No, these pages are true, as are his hateful words."

Oyana's voice cracked as she asked, "Then why tell us?"

Turning to her, the Oritheri Cowr passed the book to one of the warriors, who returned it to the desk carefully. "I tell you because you will be dead soon, and it amuses me. From time to time, when a slave is due to be put to death, I bring them here and show them this. Most disbelieve, as that one did," he pointed to Jemik without turning to face him, "but most also eventually crumble, as she has," and now he pointed at Yaletha. "Either way, it is theater most entertaining."

Oyana felt sick to her stomach, but she nevertheless added, "Is that the only reason you kept us alive?"

The Oritheri Cowr tapped his lip with a bony finger. "Well, now, there's something to that question," he said thoughtfully. "You see, we've had signs falsified before, but never three, and never before so many eyes. Your people may become restless if we do not put an end to this soon. Decisively. We will, of course, ensure no one can follow after you and falsify the Fourth Spear; men are already in place in and around the aviary. But that is not enough. There must be no doubt left in their minds that the day is *not* yet come, that it is time to lower their heads, walk softly, and obey their masters, and hope their children's children's children might one day see the Six Spears. We assume you will not willingly cooperate in this effort, so we will simply use your bodies to stage a tableau that they can discover. You'll be found amongst evidence of a scheme to falsify the signs for your own aggrandizement, and perverse pleasure. You will be shown engaging with one another in all manner of sick depravities." At this, Jemik was lunging at him, snarling, but was caught and dragged back to the wall by two of the guards. The Oritheri Cowr continued as if nothing had happened, not even missing a beat. "You will become another object lesson of the value of being peaceful and subservient, of what can go wrong to a Haebinnor who presumes too much. And your people will whisper your names to remind themselves of their need to bow and obey. In the end, you will have done almost as much to subjugate your people as the first Oritheri Cowr himself."

Chapter 12: The Fourth Spear

Had there been another moment of the gloating of the Oritheri Cowr, someone would surely have hurled himself at the smirking vizier, even at the cost of being skewered on the spear of one of the guards that attended him. Jemik was already being pressed against the wall by two warriors in full armor; Oyana, Thargoz, and even Ulgi were bristling with each contempt-laced word.

So perhaps it was fortunate that, at that moment, one wall of the tower suddenly burst inward, sand flying every which way. A huge ballista bolt, almost as wide as a tree trunk, tipped with an iron anchor, had crashed into the room and now lay across the floor; all around it, what seemed at first like ragged bricks began to unravel, sand dissipating into the air. Shattered pieces of window glass lay jaggedly all around.

One wall of the tower was now a gaping, ragged hole, which Yaletha turned to stare out, brushing sand, dust, and splinters of glass off herself. There, in the distance, perched atop the fortification wall that ringed the town, was a ballista, pointed this way. "How?" she began. Then, "Why?" Indeed, why would anyone fire a ballista at a tower inside the town, let alone this very room? The coincidence of it was simply beyond belief.

Behind her, Kumza and Thargoz were checking on their comrades. They'd all added a few more bruises, cuts, and other injuries to those they'd been accumulating since they'd seen the white-furred aurochs – was that only the day before? – but none were seriously hurt. Neither were most of the guards; a few had broken limbs, but Kumza didn't see any who might perish. And the Oritheri Cowr must have been well enough to flee; even now, the door was swinging ajar, a cowled figure disappearing down the stairs.

The flame that shrouded the tip of the ballista bolt leaped to the desk. Books and parchment scrolls of incalculable age and value began to burn, while most of those present stared in bewilderment at one another.

And at last, the guards that weren't pinned or badly injured regained their wits and began to move into position, blocking the exit and preparing to corner the slaves. Thinking quickly, Jemik snatched up a spear that one of the injured guards had dropped, and brandished it, slowing their advance. Oyana and Thargoz followed suit, while Ulgi chose a large, jagged block of wood broken from the now-burning desk. While this kept the guards at bay for now, there was nowhere for them to go. The only door was behind the guards; behind them was nothing but the wall, with its ragged hole. Which, Yaletha noted with astonishment, was starting to slowly close, like a healing wound. The ever-moving sand within the walls extended out a little farther into the gap with each moment, held in, presumably, by the winds that shaped the wall. In a few minutes, it would be sealed around the rough timber of the ballista bolt.

She was peering out the gap and down, so far, so very very far, to the ground below, when Kumza pushed into her hands one of the huge silk sheets. "Here, hold the corners," she was saying. Yaletha only stared blankly at her. "We have to jump," Kumza was saying. "Hold the corners out, like this, and the sheet will catch the air, like a bird's wings." She was frantically passing sheets to the others as well.

When Yaletha finally swallowed and leaped from the mending gap in the tower wall, she found herself, as she fell, marveling at the impossibility of it all. Not just that she was now plunging from a tower, hoping a sheet would buoy her up and break the fall. Not that she had somehow agreed to Kumza's insane plan. Nor even that a moment earlier, a ballista had broken open the tower and thus, somehow, freed them. No, it went all the way back to that day when someone had seen markings on a horse-hide. If there was an age of wonders, a time when Fate shaped the lives of men, she was sure she belonged nowhere near it. Somewhere far to the north, where fully half of the Oritheri warriors were meeting with those of dozens of other tribes to assault the Sea-Lords, that was where Fate's hand might be changing the tide of history, shifting the powers that ruled the world, fulfilling ancient oaths and ending rivalries of past ages in the clash of blood and steel.

But not here, in the life of an unimportant slave of no particular ability, strength, or courage.

A slave of no courage who had just leapt from a broken tower to fall, or fly, with nothing more than a silk sheet to save her.

Above and behind her, also suspended in the air by nothing but a silk sheet, Kumza was urging her friends to do the same. The ground was coming up quickly, but not so quickly that Yaletha didn't have a chance to sway, buoyed up by breezes, and glide towards a boulevard some distance from the tower. As she was nearing the ground, she saw, lining the avenues, people staring up at her and her companions. What a sight they must make, she thought. Some of the people had olive skin and green eyes, like her; they had paused in carrying out their master's work to gape at the bizarre sight.

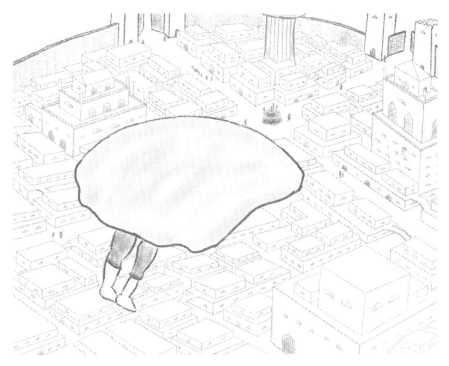

Slowly, an idea was trying to form in her mind, but the roaring of the wind, and the buffeting of the sheet above her, made it impossible for her to grasp it.

Nearer the ground, the updraft from sun-baked sand streets was stronger. At the moment she leaped, she imagined it would take mere moments to reach the ground, and indeed she'd covered half the altitude in only a dozen heartbeats, but now she was coasting on nothing but air over the top of a warehouse and making to land in a plaza nearly far enough from the tower to be out of bowshot.

"The Fourth Spear!" cried Jemik somewhere above her. "We are the birds!"

That was it. That was the idea that had been eluding her. She could see Haebinnor on the ground reaching the same conclusion, pointing, gasping, exclaiming. *The Fourth Spear shall fly, cast by a mighty bow, to shatter glass and set loose a flock of white birds across the sky of Lithgweth.* It had never been never the aviary.

The sheer absurdity of it sickened her. Or perhaps that was how quickly the ground was coming up now. She hit the cobblestones of a wide plaza, tumbled, and came up short with her back against a well, the silk sheet fluttering loose from her hands and then being carried across the courtyard by an urgent breeze.

No, she thought, this is too much. I am not a white bird. My friends are not a flock. Fate cannot play such jokes on me. I refuse to be part of such things. The stones reached up and pulled her down into the darkness.

Even when she was jostled awake, being carried on Ulgi's shoulders as her friends made a rag-tag run across the town, she felt as if she couldn't breathe and listen to them at the same time. They were talking about the idea that, while the prophecy was deliberately invented, perhaps Fate had caused it to be invented, had tricked the first Oritheri Cowr into being an unwilling prophet. Or perhaps Fate was now intervening to turn the falsehood into truth. Jemik was enthusiastic about these ideas, and as always, Thargoz

66

had to take the opposite view, insisting that some person or group was deliberately causing the signs to happen, for uncertain reasons. The very idea that such a question had to be asked nearly caused Yaletha to slip into the darkness once more.

Oritheri warriors were mobilizing to search for them, but it was a vast city, and there were many Haebinnor, and they had a considerable head start. Once while they were hiding amongst a crowd of their fellow slaves for some guards to pass, Jemik began to argue in whispered tones that they had to go, once they escaped the city, to the monument to the Oritheri Rhîs to make sure that the Fifth Spear was not prevented.

Yaletha heard someone agree with him. "Yes. It is time. Whatever Fate intends, we cannot let the Oritheri turn us into our own captors any more. We cannot let them use hope against us any longer."

What surprised her the most, and everyone else, was that the voice was hers.

Chapter 13: Rising Up

Reaching the edge of the city hadn't been easy, but it hadn't been as hard as Oyana expected. Everywhere they went, they met other Haebinnor amongst whom they could hide. In doing so, they learned how word of the Fourth Spear, and those before them, had been coursing through the Haebinnor population like a sandstorm through a forest. And in its wake were murmurs of rebellion. Had the day come? Must they make ready to rise up? Ought they be rising up already? She heard some discussing where to obtain improvised weapons, others advising caution or simply fear, and more than anything, slaves discussing who amongst them could go to the memorial to the Oritheri Rhîs, so they could see if the Fifth Spear would take place as foretold.

At first, the other Haebinnor did not recognize them, and Oyana thought it would be best to leave it that way. In a city this large, the slaves would not all know one another, so a group of unfamiliar Haebinnor would be assumed to be slaves from a remote quarter. But when Jemik, fool that he was, started to proclaim "Make way for the First Hand!" Oyana groaned and nearly struck herself out of frustration. She should have seen this coming and tried to prevent it.

Those who heard his cry seemed to believe it. Even here in Lithgweth, rumors had arrived of the sightings of the first three Spears. Some had even heard tales of the First Hand. While no one here knew Yaletha on sight, what little they'd heard fit her appearance. And she was being seen amongst them just as the Fourth Spear had been witnessed, in a fashion no one had ever expected, a most extraordinary fashion. The sort of thing that could only be explained by the hand of Fate itself. Thus, few doubted Jemik; instead, they cheered them as they passed, and offered to aid them, to clear a path for them, to rise up and follow them to battle. Despite that there were yet two Spears to be seen, some seemed to want to follow the First Hand to the palace to slay the Oritheri Baugcaun with their bare hands that very moment.

By encouraging these erstwhile followers to help them pass, Oyana was able to lead her company to sight of one of the gates, without a fight. Each time they'd seen guards they could simply melt into the crowd of slaves and pass, or wait while eager-to-please Haebinnor created a distraction. But while this was enough for the sand-white avenues, it wouldn't get them through the gate.

It was true that the Oritheri were in disarray. Some were scrambling to figure out how a ballista had been commandeered and fired on, of all things, the palace of the Oritheri Baugcaun. Others were hurrying to recall the massed army of thousands of warriors on the plains outside the city, who'd been making ready to march, to join their fellows marching to the siege of the Sea-Lords. And the Oritheri had all seen the same remarkable events as had the Haebinnor. Oyana couldn't guess what they thought these portents meant; did all the Oritheri know the prophecy's true provenance, or only some? Either way, these signs would be baffling and alarming.

But notwithstanding all these distractions, it only took a few warriors to man one of the well-designed gates and prevent a few unarmed slaves from escaping. A short Haebinnor with bulging eyes was proclaiming to Yaletha, and a dozen other slaves nearby, that they should rush the gate to make an opening by which the First Hand and her companions could escape the city. Oyana was trying to argue against this. She didn't wish to see these bystanders perish needlessly on the spears of the gate-guards in service of a hastily-conceived plan, without at least trying to think of a way to get by without needless bloodshed. It was one thing to lead her people to battle in the uprising she felt more and more sure was coming, knowing many would die in brave sacrifice for the freedom of their children. That was the sort of thing she felt she could do better than Yaletha ever could, why Fate should have chosen her to be the First Hand. But it was another to see a dozen tired men and women die for her, right in front of her, because she hadn't had time to think of a better tactic.

But events were moving too quickly. Jemik was in his element now, rallying people and inspiring them to act. That they were going to seize the first action that occurred to them, rather than one chosen wisely, was why Jemik must never be allowed to lead without someone wiser at his side. Before she could marshal her will and make her voice heard, a hunk of wood, broken off of a market stall's tent-pole, was being hurled at the guards, and there was screaming and running. Blood was already falling onto the shining white boulevard, where it pooled, as the sandstorm-winds that formed the streets refused to absorb it.

There was nothing else to do but brandish the spear she'd stolen from a guard earlier, and charge forward, trying to keep Yaletha safely between her and Thargoz. Ahead, Ulgi was roaring, with Kumza on his shoulders, counting on Oritheri guards to hesitate just a moment before standing in the way of a behemoth like him. And at the vanguard of it all, Jemik was drinking up the sheer chaos, the enthusiasm of those he was leading, probably to their deaths.

When at last the city was behind them, Oyana turned to make sure none of her company had been left behind or badly injured, but she tried not to notice how many slaves had fallen to purchase their escape. Oritheri warriors were brave and fierce; they were well armored and bore spears, axes, and bows with which they'd trained assiduously. The Haebinnor were many in number; with so many Oritheri away in the wars in the north, the Haebinnor easily outnumbered their captors. But they were barefoot, unarmed, untrained, and unprotected. A man in armor could hold off a dozen of them and take no injuries if he did not blanch. Though she tried not to, time and again Oyana saw Haebinnor blood, and she finally gave up and took it all in. There were at least four who had died, and many more were injured. One of these, Ulgi was carrying, and Kumza on his shoulders was leaning over his head to bind the wounds even while they trundled forward.

They couldn't linger even here, outside the gates. Even if the Oritheri hadn't realized who they were, the mere fact that they were runaway slaves, who'd been involved in an act of insurrection, would be cause enough to chase them. That one of them was being hailed as the First Hand would make the hunters all the more determined. Oyana thought to suggest a direction, then changed her mind. She turned to Yaletha. "Do we make way towards the Fifth Spear, Yaletha?" she asked.

There was a moment while the others paused, drinking in the fact that Oyana had just deferred to Yaletha. For a moment she thought Jemik might start insisting on a course of action, and then Thargoz would oppose him, and Yaletha would let the argument decide for her, or grind the whole fellowship to a stop. But instead, Jemik nodded. "Indeed, shall we? I think we should, but I will follow where you lead, First Hand," he said. And Thargoz, by his posture and his silence, seemed to agree as well.

It took Yaletha only a moment to answer. "I do not know if, when we arrive, we shall be trying to cause the Fifth Spear, or prevent it from being averted, or if we go merely to witness it. I would welcome your thoughts on this matter. But whichever it may be, we must make haste. The hounds will be on our trail. More than that, our people will soon be hurling themselves into untimely rebellion. Whether prophecy tells us this dooms us or not, it's senseless for them to die needlessly. If they have some sign to witness, some First Hand to follow, at least that may check their fervor, hold their strike until a better moment."

Oyana was surprised at how decisive this was. But as they loped towards the distant slope from which, amongst frail pines, rose the statue of the long-dead Oritheri Rhîs, she turned Yaletha's words over in her thoughts, and was surprised what she found. Once she looked past the clarity and determination, it was clear that Yaletha's answer was just another way to avoid her fate, to seek quiet. She'd chosen a path that freed her from having to lead, having to choose. Perhaps she'd started to accept that she was the First Hand, but she was only using it to diminish the prominence of that very role.

As they ran, Jemik, Kumza, and Thargoz discussed amongst them what might cause or prevent the Fifth Spear, or what it could even mean – if the sky itself would cast it, what could anyone do to make it happen, or not happen? But Oyana did not enter into the discussion. Instead, she stared into the stormy skies ahead, and frowned. If there was to be a rebellion, and it seemed more likely every passing hour, how could it triumph if the First Hand was still turning away from difficult choices? If the Haebinnor might win their freedom, it would be bought with much blood. If she was reluctant to spill it when needed, they could not hope to ever be free.

Chapter 14: The Fifth Spear

The monument to the Oritheri Rhîs was more than a league away, but the trip was more arduous than its distance, as the ground sloped upward nearly the whole way. Lithgweth sat at the southwest of a great valley of plains, a shallow bowl whose open fields were heavily used as pastureland and farms. The city, and the roads leading east from it towards the lands of other kings, served as the southern border of this valley. The north and west were bounded by a ridge of hills, gentle mounds at the southwestern end of the ridge, then curving north and east in a great arc, reaching heights at the eastern end that might be called mountains, at least by someone who had never seen the vast peaks in the west. Midway along this arc, perched atop the ridge, were the ruins of the king's city. It had grown up from a defensive fortress, located on a high hilltop to be defensible and for its commanding views of the valley. But this also made it vulnerable to sandstorms that swept across the pasture; and now all that remained were tumbled stones, and the partially-shattered Spire of Last Days.

Much farther west and south, the ridge was little more than a line of hills, atop which grew the only true forest in the area. Mostly scrappy pines with a sprinkling of hornbeams, elms, and slender oaks, this woodland was visited only by lumberjacks, save for the path leading to the statue of the Oritheri Rhîs. It presided atop the peak of one of the highest of these hills, in a clearing where grew flowers of all sorts.

The queen had come from far west, given by her father to the Oritheri Baugcaun to strengthen ties between two kingdoms. Her heart longed for the flowers and trees of her home, and when she found this glade of wildflowers, she took to visiting it nearly every day. Thus it was that, when she was claimed by the sandstorm that destroyed the city, the bereaved Oritheri Baugcaun ordered her glade preserved and beautified, and had a monument built to her, standing tall above it, to watch over her beloved blossoms forever. This monument, along with the aviary that housed her doves, had long been points of contention amongst the Oritheri. Some saw them as a wasteful extravagance, carrying out whimsies for someone long past, while those still alive suffered; others saw them as a small concession to peace, beauty, and tranquility in an otherwise harsh land and culture.

As she tried to force her weary body to climb the comparatively gentle slope leading towards those hills, Yaletha pondered how the Fourth Spear had seemed to refer to one of these two monuments, while the Fifth Spear to the other. Long habit made her first take the prophecy at face value, and wonder if they had merely misinterpreted the Fifth Spear, as they had the Fourth. Then the memory of its falsehood, of the lie that had been the core of her life and the lives of every other Haebinnor for centuries, crashed in on her again. After she'd reeled from that for the hundredth time, she considered the coincidence of two Spears referring to two monuments in the light of its true provenance. The Oritheri Rhîs had perished only a decade before the creation of the prophecy; the building of the aviary and statue were fresh on the minds of everyone then, including the first Oritheri Cowr. And in the minds of the Haebinnor who he intended to deceive with it. Using the monuments was just another way to twist their thoughts in a direction to his liking, by giving them an interpretation that seemed mysterious, yet was easily reached, and had just the right amount of impossibility.

There were, no doubt, Oritheri hunters behind them. But there were scores, no, hundreds, of other Haebinnor here, nearly all of them runaways. Some were gathering in the western pastureland, from which the monument was little more than a dark spot on a distant ridge; others were traveling, as she was, towards the base of the hills, to get closer to it. The Oritheri hounds were keeping a distance; there were too few of them to deal with so many slaves in brazen defiance. She'd heard word that, to the east, the army of the Oritheri that had been readying to march north was now gathering. They were at least a thousand in number, and she wondered what their absence might mean to their fellows, and allies, in the invasions being readied in faraway lands. But she felt sure it meant

76

the end of her people, here and now. If all the Haebinnor in Lithgweth, and many more from other settlements, gathered here, they might well outnumber the Oritheri army by nearly ten to one. But they were barefoot slaves. It would take all of them, acting as one, and undiminished by fear or hesitation, to pose a threat to an army.

Night was falling as they reached the base of the hill. They had not slept or eaten in days, and had hardly had a moment's rest; continuing towards the monument was out of the question. Dozens of other Haebinnor had made a campsite there, and they were entirely welcoming to any of their kind wishing to join them. A few had brought some food, while others had gathered some of the meager forage and hunt the hills offered, and these too they shared with open arms.

There was a quality to the moment that struck Yaletha as unreal: sitting in apparent peace and freedom with a few dozen of her people, almost fearless of the Oritheri, living as if this had always been their lot in life. They worked together readily, setting up guard duty and dividing up the labor of keeping the camp. They laughed, they talked, and sometimes they even sang. At times it filled Yaletha with hope, but fleetingly; soon she would be back to dreading the moment when the axe fell, as it seemed it must. And dreading even more her role. The role forced on her. The First Hand.

While the other slaves discussed possible interpretations of the Fifth Spear, what form a spear cast by the sky might take, Yaletha pondered how she had become the First Hand. Something or someone was causing the events of a false prophecy to come true, and the first of these was a sign that pointed to her. *The First Hand shall fell, trembling, a beast of noble blood, within whose very flesh will be scribed a spear circled; and thus shall the First Spear be seen, and the First Hand known.* Why her? She'd wondered this since that first day, in the Court of the Well, and all that had been learned since had changed the meaning of the question, but not its intent. Was it Fate, and if so, why would it choose so unsuitable a First Hand? Or might one of the Oritheri have chosen her to intentionally sabotage the hope of freedom by starting the events of the prophecy along, but crippling it with a hopeless choice of a First Hand? But then how would the Oritheri Cowr not know of such an effort?

For that matter, how could one falsify such a sign? She recalled that the horse had, so the tale had gone, come from a faraway land in the train of a wandering merchant, and had been sold to the Oritheri Cowr when it was a full-grown stallion, selected for its fiery temperament, strength, and speed. Could the man who sold it have somehow shaped the beast's growth to create the pattern? Or simply found one horse that would already have such a shape, then brought it here? If so, that she became the First Hand was mere chance; she just happened to be the slave assigned to such duty in the town where the horse's remains were sold. Had the horse died two years earlier, it would have been another, and had it died two years later, perhaps someone else. And while her master was the most prominent trade in horse-flesh in this land, he was not the only one; the horse might have gone to another. Many hands might have become the First Hand, instead of hers. Perhaps another was meant to be, by Fate or by a mysterious merchant, and chance steered this plan awry.

No matter how she turned these thoughts over in her mind, they circled back on each other like the marking in the hide. They followed her down the well of exhaustion and chased one another within her troubled dreams, full of the sounds of a rising storm, or a roaring horde, or the clash of axe against bone. She stumbled in a moonless darkness through the roaring, to an end she could not see. Her friends would sometimes approach, looming out of the pitch-black night, but always they tried to push or pull her, and she could not know if the direction they chose was the right one. Now Thargoz was pulling insistently on her hand, but did he wish to guide her to safety, or heroics, or to his bed, or simply around some footfall in the darkness? He grew more and more urgent, and finally she awoke to find him pulling her hand, saying, "Awaken, Yaletha, we must be away! Oritheri approach!"

She expected on rising to see the entire army, clad in shining armor, charging from the plains and ready to swoop down upon them with a thousand shining axes red with Haebinnor blood. But her eyes were met by only a few dozen Oritheri hunters, moving from one camp to another to try to stir up fear and break up unity amongst the slaves as much as they could, so the army's strike, if it were needed, would go that much more easily. Oyana explained to Yaletha, as they hurried up the hill and through the pines to avoid them, how a few such squads of Oritheri were scattering groups of Haebinnor all around the valley. In some cases it was working; bereft by fear, some slaves were turning themselves in, returning to the city, or running away in simple terror. In others, groups of Haebinnor were banding together to hold off the Oritheri hounds. Thus far, there had been little bloodshed, but it was only a matter of time.

There was a path leading up to the clearing, but they avoided it, because many more Oritheri were hurrying up it. "They know what Spear is next as well," Oyana mused, "and there are warriors and guards gathering in the clearing, to prevent us from reaching it, or for some other purpose." The roaring from her dream continued to haunt Yaletha; she thought it was just in her ears until she saw Ulgi wince at a sudden roll of thunder. Far above them, rain was falling, but the pines kept them dry. "Look, there, another dozen or so. No one will be able to get anywhere near the monument," Oyana continued, but Yaletha was having trouble paying attention. The rain seemed wrong somehow. Storms like this struck from time to time; the land wasn't dry because it never rained, it was dry because it rarely rained, but when it did, it did so prodigiously. At this time of year, a thunderstorm would be a welcome relief to the farmers and cattle-ranchers on the pastureland behind them. What seemed wrong about it? Yaletha couldn't focus enough to answer the question, or even frame it clearly.

The sight as they reached the edge of the clearing was enough to make Yaletha's eyes go wide. She'd never seen the statue itself, nor the plaza surrounding it, fashioned from cut stone in a bewildering variety of colors, arranged in pattern that seemed

79

random at first, but nevertheless, immediately pleasing to the eye. Nor had she ever seen this many flowers before. In the time of the Oritheri Rhîs, wildflowers had grown here, but now, it was a carefully tended garden, with neatly arranged blooms positioned to create shapes delineated by gradations of hue, breathtakingly beautiful even in the half-light of the growing storm. The statue itself towered over it all, a sublime representation of a serene woman with a small songbird on her hand, carved by a master at the art of shaping stone.

But all the perfect asymmetries and artistic flourishes were pushed aside by the ugliness around it. Forming a ring around the statue, arm to arm and spear to shield, were nearly a hundred Oritheri warriors. Outside this ring, dozens of other Oritheri were working in small groups, driving tall iron stakes into the ground, and linking them one to the other with the sort of steel chain used in fashioning ballistae.

Hanging back in the cover of the tree-line, they stared at this a few moments. "If that's a fence to keep us out," Jemik mused, "it seems a bit much. I'd think those soldiers will do the job quite well."

"Perhaps they mean to use a fence for a lengthier occupation," Thargoz mused. "The Fifth Spear might not happen today, but if it happened three days hence, that would still be a threat. They can't spare a hundred soldiers to stand in a ring indefinitely."

"If that's to be a fence," objected Oyana, "it's a poor one. The posts are too far apart, and much too high. Even Ulgi could walk under the chain."

Kumza was starting to say something when Thargoz answered, "It might just be the start of some construction. Perhaps there are more materials being brought here. They have had to move hastily to arrive here before we did."

"I think I know..." Kumza began, but Jemik spoke over her. "If that's how they're starting, they clearly don't know a thing about building fences. They should have gotten us to build it. I know a woman back home who builds fences for her mistress who could show them a thing or two."

Before Kumza could make another try, Oyana asked, "That's a fair point, though, if this is manual labor, why not bring some slaves to do it?"

"Because they're afraid they'd do it poorly. Many of us are in open rebellion," Thargoz said. "What is it?" he finally said to Kumza.

But before she could answer, there was a blinding flash and a sound like the world shattering. When their eyes cleared, there was a scorch-spot on the far side of the clearing, and all the Oritheri workers had stepped away from the chains. "That's what it is," Kumza finally said over the ringing in their ears. "They place these on high towers. When lightning strikes, these iron stakes catch it and carry it down the chain to the ground, so the tower itself is unharmed. They're building a large net of them to protect the statue," she continued thoughtfully, "because they've come to the same conclusion Thargoz did, that a spear cast by the sky might be a bolt of lightning. Particularly given this," she concluded, gesturing to the angry storm-clouds above.

They were silent for a time as they considered this. Yaletha remembered noticing such stakes, though she'd never known what they were for. Now she could recall a storm-cloud gliding over the city back home, and lightning striking near one of the towers, time and again. Something about the memory of that storm struck her as odd. No, it wasn't that. The storm above them now was odd. How did it differ from the ones she recalled?

Everyone seemed to be afraid to ask the next question: what now? Only a few days earlier both they and the Oritheri were trying to work in secret, but now, on the plain below them, hundreds, perhaps thousands, of Haebinnor stared up into the storm in open defiance, while an army of Oritheri waited, champing at the bit, to strike them down. Here the Oritheri efforts to stop the Fifth Spear were flagrant; they were growing desperate, perhaps, but their efforts seemed to be unstoppable. Several times, another lightning strike arced from the sky and kissed one of the iron stakes, causing them to flinch or even cry out in the ensuing thunderclap.

One such lightning-stroke, particularly close, brought with it a flash of understanding to Yaletha. Every time she'd seen such a storm, it had rolled in from the east. She did not know why; perhaps the source of thunderstorms was in the lands east of them, or perhaps something in the shape of the land drove them that way. But this storm, alone of all she'd ever witnessed, was moving from the west.

The same lightning-stroke sparked an idea in Jemik's mind, but unlike Yaletha, Jemik moved directly from thought to speech. "That's it! We steal one of those stakes and bring it up onto the statue. Plant it there, and it will capture the spear cast from the sky into the statue."

Oyana stared at him in disbelief a moment, which allowed Thargoz to be the one to say, "And how exactly can the six of us overpower a dozen Oritheri to steal a stake, then hold off a hundred more while one of us climbs up a statue, in a rainstorm?"

"We only have to buy her a few minutes," Jemik answered excitedly. "We move quickly. They won't be expecting it. We circle to that point there, then dash across, snatching up stakes as we go. Then we charge at those soldiers there, by the right foot. We just have to startle them a few moments and she can climb up onto the foot. Then they won't be able to catch up if they try to follow. They'd be climbing in heavy armor."

"She?" Yaletha asked, though she was fairly sure she knew what Jemik meant. But no one listened to her question.

"Even if we could," Thargoz objected, "they have spears. And some have bows. She'd be out in the open, unprotected."

"Then we have to keep fighting," Jemik concluded. "Keep them too busy, or too far away. We cannot win that fight, but we don't need to. We only have to buy her a few moments."

"Buy who a few moments?" Yaletha objected. The idea of climbing up a set of stairs set her slightly ill at ease. Climbing a smooth stone statue, made slick by a thunderstorm, while carrying an iron stake, set her heart to racing. And below her, her friends would be dying to ensure that spears being thrown at her might happen to miss? She couldn't even muster the words to object. She wasn't even sure if she was asking these questions aloud; no one seemed to be noticing them.

"We wouldn't last a dozen heartbeats, let alone long enough for her to reach the arm," Oyana was saying. "If you recall, we tried this plan once before, buying her time to ride into the aurochs herd, and against only a few Oritheri with the element of surprise, and with them not realizing what we were doing, we scarcely managed it. And got put into chains for the effort."

"We have to try!" Jemik shouted, loud enough that a few of the Oritheri tilted their heads, but it didn't matter, because he was now charging out into the clearing at full tilt towards a pile of iron stakes, and the Oritheri who were assembling them.

He might have reached them before the stunned Oritheri could react, if the flowers hadn't been drenched by the storm. His bare feet found little purchase in a sea of sodden buttercups, and he went over backwards, feet flying up into the air, and landed in a thin puddle, causing a damp thud and a splash.

It was so incongruous that some of the Oritheri broke into laughter. And though she would deny it later, Oyana also let out a small giggle. Just for a moment, before the terrible gravity of the situation came down on her. Already, the Oritheri were staring in their direction. Spears were being leveled, and warriors moving into formation. Oyana decided to suppress the giggle, but it had already fled of its own accord. "Thargoz, see if you can grab him and pull him back to the tree-line. Kumza, stay with Yaletha, protect her. Make her run if this goes badly. Ulgi, you and I move to flank to defend him while he does. Quickly!" And she was already moving. Only a heartbeat later everyone else was following her orders, and after a few moments more, spears were being splintered, blood was being spilled in the rain, and there were heavy thumps of bodies striking the hard, damp soil.

Yaletha was hardly noticing any of it. Her eyes were fixed on the statue. There at the top, in a flicker of lightning, she'd seen movement, and was staring so as not to miss it in the next flash. There! A figure was perched atop a giant stone shoulder. She could make out nothing but a cloak and hood, and an iron stake, being bound to the statue; then the dark swallowed it. She stared until her eyes ached, longing for another stroke of light, but when it came, she saw only the stake; the figure was gone.

Oyana and Thargoz were grunting a few feet in front of her, dragging a huge shape. Kumza was shrieking. She felt arms go around her, and numbly she fought them off, but only because she had to see. Who was it? What was it? Lightning might strike again and she wouldn't see! She heard Jemik's voice very nearby, saying something about retreating. It must have been his arms she was flailing against. Where was Ulgi? Who was that atop the statue? What was he doing, and to what end?

And as she wondered this, the world opened up, and light poured out of it. She imagined she could see it reaching down, like the hand of a lover coming down from the sky to gently caress a cheek. But the cheek belonged to the Oritheri Rhîs, and the caress was ungentle.

Stone was flying every which way. Scores of Oritheri warriors, who'd been standing just below the statue, were pelted by boulders of sizes ranging from a grain of rice to a plough-horse. Crumpled bodies were scattered all around the remains of the statue. There was no sound: the thunderclap, and the shattering of the monument, had taken it away. Yaletha was now being dragged back into the woods. People were silently screaming.

As sound began to return, she heard the clamoring of the voices of her friends, urging them to escape before the Oritheri could regroup. Behind her, there was a deep roar, which she would later realize was made of the voices of thousands of Haebinnor, many thousands, arrayed haphazardly across the pasturelands, cheering. But all this meant nothing to Yaletha. All she could see now was the memory of a half-glimpsed silhouette of a figure standing atop a statue's shoulder, shrouded in a cloak. All her questions pointed to that figure, now swallowed by the night.

Chapter 15: Last Days

Too much was happening; Kumza struggled to block it all out. She needed to clear her thoughts, to focus, but the camp was a tempest of words and feelings, fears and wants. There were people all around, moving every which way, and each one trailed a whirlwind of ideas, emotions, dreads, desires, and anxieties. The number of people afforded some safety; that's why they'd stopped here, at this camp near the edge of the hills. But of all these people, Kumza was the only one who could spare more than a few thoughts for Ulgi. "Please," she said, trying to make it a forceful demand but fearing it had come out like a pained, mousy plea instead, "please give us some room."

She'd always counted on Ulgi to be the one to make space for her. Even on an ordinary day, it was easy for the constant hum of people around her, talking, feeling, wanting, hurting, and a thousand other things, to overwhelm her with a constant stream of impressions she had never been able to close herself to, like others could. She didn't think she was any better than anyone else at knowing the secret wishes and fears of others; she just couldn't *not* know them. When she needed some escape, Ulgi provided it. All he had to do was draw himself to his full height and perhaps bellow, and people stepped aside, sometimes not even realizing why.

Of course, he contributed his own stream of thoughts and feelings, but they were simple, honest, direct, and ultimately soothing to her. She had never known anyone more honest. People imagined his thoughts were simplistic, and in some ways they were, though not as much as they imagined. He had more wit than they gave credit for. What he lacked was the layers of lies and trickery, and especially, of self-deception. The feelings that washed over Kumza from others were encrusted with layers of anxiety, fear, want, anger, and hurt, most of which they were not aware of, or did not admit. The smallest utterance from Yaletha was but a hint of the maelstrom below it, but Ulgi's feelings were a soothing brook, direct and comfortable. No one else really understood this, and thus, why Kumza and Ulgi belonged together so well.

Yaletha made a half-hearted attempt to encourage the other Haebinnor in the area to step away and quiet their voices, which didn't help nearly enough, but Kumza was appreciative anyway. She could still hear and feel their discussions, but she had enough room to lean over the supine hulk of Ulgi, confront the deluge of her own feelings, and take his hand. It was almost cold, which wasn't a good sign. He was going into shock; he'd lost a lot of blood. Her hands quaked as she changed his bandages, wishing she had better, cleaner rags to use. His eyes fluttered open a moment, then closed again. "Please," she repeated, more yearningly, only to him. But he was beyond the reach of her words.

Behind her was the constant low roar of thousands of Haebinnor gathered on the west side of the valley, and more pouring in all the time. From what she'd overheard, Lithgweth was almost emptied of slaves, and many more had come from the surrounding farms and ranches, from nearby settlements, even some from more remote cities. She expected that, somewhere in the throng, there were scores of slaves from her own home, people she knew. People who would soon be bleeding, perhaps dying. Like her beloved was.

Most of the chatter was, of course, about the Six Spears. Each sign had erased some of the doubt, and the Fifth Spear, occurring before many eyes despite organized Oritheri efforts to stop it, had erased the last of the doubt in all but her own company. Somehow, the fact that the Oritheri clearly knew the prophecy, and that according to that prophecy that meant they were doomed, was being overlooked by all. There was a sense that the moment to seize freedom was now or never. But it was more than that. Surely there were Haebinnor who believed that, according to the prophecy, they were doomed, *sand in their breath*. But those would not have come here to the fight. They might be cowering in the cities, hoping to survive the doom, or at least to die more peacefully.

In a strange reversal, while nearly everyone around him had the same certainty that was Jemik's natural state, he himself was having doubts, perhaps for the first time. He hadn't seen the figure Yaletha saw on the statue; no one saw it but her. But she spoke with utter conviction, and Kumza could tell she was being truthful. That lightning had struck the statue, after the net of stakes had protected it so many times, gave everyone else reason to believe her.

"If it were a Haebinnor, why would he push us towards a war we cannot win?" Yaletha protested. They'd been trying to figure out who the figure might have been. "Either he believes in the prophecy, or he doesn't. If he does, why force us to act, even after it's plain the Oritheri know of the Six Spears? And if he does not, what is his reason to take such steps in the first place?"

"Mayhap he wants to see us rise and throw off our chains, and thinks by this to inspire us to do so," Thargoz answered, but he didn't seem convinced. "See how, for the first time, thousands of us move without the fear of the lash, acting together." He waved a hand at the crowd stretching before them into the distance; the rising sun was starting to illumine the masses, casting long shadows towards them.

"But how could a Haebinnor manage it?" Oyana asked. "He would have to have been on the statue even before the Oritheri arrived, with a stake ready, hiding."

"That's true no matter who it is," Jemik insisted. "He could have been hidden in the folds of the statue's cloak, by the shoulder. Unless someone specifically looked, they wouldn't notice."

"But that only would help if he knew a storm was coming," Oyana was saying, which made Yaletha's eyes widen. "And how would they have..."

"The storm!" Yaletha cried out, making Kumza wince. She turned back to Ulgi. Fishing around in her tattered clothes, she withdrew a tiny phial. In it was an unguent she'd been saving for the most dire of injuries. She held it up in the thin light of dawn, and glanced over her shoulder at thousands of her people. Many of them would need treatment like this soon; she agonized over whether to use some for Ulgi, who, due to his size and injuries, would need as much of it as would serve three, four, maybe five other injured people. The ache of this decision was threatening to overwhelm her even more than Yaletha's welter of anxieties.

"What about the storm?" Thargoz asked, curiously. He looked up at the sky. There was nothing now but a few tattered clouds, trailing away in an odd jumble.

"It came from the west," Yaletha pronounced.

"So?"

"Storms like that always come from the east here," she said with exaggerated impatience. "Could it be that… the person on the statue… called the storm?"

"No one can call storms," Thargoz protested.

"That's not true," Oyana said, glancing over at Kumza. "Were we not, just yesterday, in a city that was essentially made from a storm, not only called but contained and shaped? The Crimson Sorcerers are able to do many things, and shaping the weather as you might shape wood or stone is not beyond them."

"What purpose could a sorcerer have to climb the statue and falsify the signs?" Yaletha was asking. "Could one cause a beast's hide to grow in a particular shape?"

Thargoz stroked his chin thoughtfully. "That needs no sorcery. Anyone could, if they were patient enough, and had access to enough horses. It might take years, or even generations of horses, but if you created just a very tiny scar along a muscle's fold, and did this for dozens of horses, at least one or two would develop the right pattern. You might not be able to tell which one, though. So you'd have to sell them all. And there'd be no way to know who might butcher the right one, and thus, become the First Hand." He gave Yaletha a sympathetic look. "Falsifying the Third Spear would be easier. You said that the white fur seemed unhealthy. That could be because the aurochs was treated with dyes to give it the right color and pattern."

"And we already heard that there were signs of the Second Spear being falsified," Oyana agreed. "Moktig claimed there'd been indications the tree had been transplanted to the bog. You only would have to wait for a sandstorm in the east and then transplant it before moonrise."

"Seizing a ballista in Lithgweth would be more challenging," Thargoz was continuing, while Yaletha was practically hopping from foot to foot. "But not impossible. And we already know someone could make their way here, steal an iron stake, and place it on the statue. Even Jemik was able to think up *that* plan."

"But not early enough," Jemik conceded in a rare moment of self-deprecation.

"However, bringing in a storm… only a sorcerer could do that, I think," Thargoz concluded.

"Or someone who was working with a sorcerer. For all we know, the man on the statue was only one of several working together."

"Which would explain how they could move so quickly," Oyana added, nodding. "If the man who fired that ballista was also the one who climbed the statue, he would have needed a swift steed and a spot of luck, to be in place in time. But one might be preparing for one Spear while another is carrying out the previous."

Kumza was only half-listening, in fact trying to shut it all out, but even so, every word, every thought, every feeling was making its impression on her. Still, she was mostly staring at the phial. "I will need him," she whispered to herself, "to help me hold this camp for healing. Many will soon need my abilities, but if there is not a safe place to which they can be brought, it won't matter how much unguent I have left. They cannot spare anyone to guard it who can fight, but Ulgi, if he's well enough to stand, could defend it through his intimidating bulk, even if he cannot fight." Part of her knew she was finding reasons to support the decision her heart had already made, and unlike most people, she couldn't silence that part of her, nor choose not to hear it. But while it called her selfish, she opened the phial and carefully spread the precious tincture of herbs across his injuries.

"Do you suppose one of them is already atop the Spire of Last Days?" Yaletha was asking.

"It doesn't matter," Oyana answered. "The prophecy still requires you to be the one there, to raise the Sixth Spear. Everyone here, across the entire valley, will be able to see it happening."

"And the Oritheri will know we mean to make for it," Thargoz added. "They will be moving to stop us, if they have not already."

Kumza couldn't hear some of what followed, while they made preparations, because Ulgi was stirring. He even managed to sit up, only to sink back down as she threw herself against him to embrace him tightly. "We're staying here to heal the hurt," she whispered to him, "and you're forbidden from doing anything more than trying to scare people away."

"Did get friends safe away from stone woman?" Ulgi asked, interrupting himself frequently for gulps of air.

"For now," she answered. "But they are heading for the Spire of Last Days now. And I see why it is called that. No matter what happens next, whether we all fall under the axe, sand in our breath, or we triumph and become free, this is the last day of the life we have known."

Chapter 16: The Heart's Voice

Yaletha objected the most strenuously to Kumza and Ulgi being left behind. The others could see the sense in it. Ulgi was in no condition to travel, let alone fight. Had he not had a talented healer beside him, he would likely have perished by now. And Kumza's arts would be needed more here than on the path to the Spire of Last Days. Still, it was a tearful parting, and Yaletha embraced them both tightly before accepting it. Kumza took the opportunity to whisper to her. "I don't know if fate is ours to shape, or we are fate's to shape; but either way, Yaletha, you *must* accept it. Your heart tells you always what you wish, what is right for you. I can hear it, even when you can't. You must let it speak to you."

There was a winding path up the hillside that led from the valley towards the Spire of Last Days, the ruins of the road that once led to the old city. Jemik took the lead as they set out across the pastureland towards the foot of the path. They passed through camps of dozens of Haebinnor, who had come to see the Fifth Spear, and who now were milling aimlessly, simply waiting to see the Sixth. Many hadn't planned to join a war for their freedom, and many still didn't realize such a fight was nigh-inevitable. They'd always imagined, from the way the prophecy was worded, that after the Sixth Spear the Oritheri would simply be gone, their works rent unto dust, without any further toil or struggle.

But knowing the true origin of the prophecy, Yaletha ached at the sight of these people, so innocent of what must come next. Many of these people would die. More would bear injuries that would last a lifetime. Some would kill, which could be a terrible burden to bear in its own way. The thousand warriors to the east were prepared; they bore spears and axes which had already tasted blood. The slaves had no better weapons than the stones at their feet, and had never faced the terror of battle. They had no order, no direction, no leadership. Even when it was clear their choices were to fight or to die, they would mill about, like lost foals, and be cut down on the very cusp of their liberation. It gnawed at Yaletha's heart. She wondered if it weren't too late to surrender and bring this all to an end, to go back to how it was, just to spare them.

Kumza's words still buzzed in her ear, and she turned over her choices, trying to let her heart tell her which was the right one. She knew this had gone too far to be stopped. Even if the mysterious figure she'd seen took no more steps, the Haebinnor in the fields would not return meekly to their servitude, nor would the Oritheri accept it if they did, without some grand demonstration. There must be a battle. And if there must, someone must lead it, or the Haebinnor would be slain to the last, dust in their breath.

Every time her thoughts came to this point, her knees weakened, and she felt trapped like a beast in a cage, on the edge of panic. She was, like it or not, the First Hand. But the idea of trying to lead her people to battle was simply beyond consideration. She didn't need Kumza's words of wisdom to see that she could not be a war-leader, that it was not in her heart to do it. But the need for leadership was inescapable.

Around and around she chased these questions, and when she finally found the answer, she nearly fell over on the stones at the base of the path. Oyana caught her, but before she could ask what was wrong, Yaletha said breathlessly, "Let us pause a moment and speak on what is to come next."

From here they had a better view of the masses arrayed in the valley. With half the Oritheri army far away preparing to strike the hated Sea-Lords, and nearly every Haebinnor within a week's journey now here in the valley, they outnumbered their enemy by more than five to one. But five unarmed, undisciplined slaves could offer little threat to an Oritheri warrior. She nearly blanched at that thought, but gathered the tatters of her courage around her like a cloak, and spoke in a voice that was nearly steady.

"Look you upon our people. They march to war, though most know it not. They expect the prophecy to whisk them to freedom without their stir, but we know the truth of the prophecy. This day shall not

94

end but with blood, even if the Sixth Spear be raised." She paused a moment, then, murmuring Kumza's words to herself, she fanned the spark of her conviction and continued. "Someone must lead them into this fight. I had long thought that it must be the First Hand, and I cannot do it. But that is not what the prophecy has been telling us all along. The First Hand raises the Sixth Spear, up there," she pointed to the Spire above them, "but the battle will be fought *here*, in the valley. The prophecy does not demand I command the army; in fact, it insists that I cannot. No, that burden falls to you. Some of you must stay here, to lead this makeshift army."

"What?" Thargoz protested. "No, we must see to the Sixth Spear first. I shall not leave your side."

Her determination was fragile. It was scarcely a month since she would have hidden from any disagreement; and just two days earlier, she still would not have dared to voice a contrary opinion. But that life had ended, and the world had reshaped itself around her. She clung to Kumza's admonition. "It is necessary. They must be led, and I will be atop the Spire at the moment of their need. I can feel this," she placed a hand over her heart, "to be true. Tell me you do not see the wisdom in it?"

Oyana's eyes had widened at first, but now they grew bright. "She is correct," she said. "I have been at a loss for what my part in this might be. I've tried to help the First Hand, but part of me felt like I had some other role to play, and could not find what it was. For a time I thought I ought to have been the First Hand, but now it is clear." She put her hands together before her chest and bowed to Yaletha in a formal pose. "It would be my honor to serve the First Hand thus."

Thargoz looked ever the more troubled. "No!" he protested. "We will all be needed to reach the Spire. I say again, I shall not leave your side, Yaletha!"

"It will do us no good to reach the Spire if our people simply wander into slaughter," Yaletha explained patiently to Thargoz. "The

95

prophecy cannot guarantee that merely raising the Sixth Spear will cast the Oritheri down, until not one grain stands atop another. The prophecy is false, and even if it were not, our people will still have to win their victory with courage and blood. Nor can we assume our mysterious benefactors will intervene; how could they lead the people to victory? We cannot even be sure that is their desired outcome. The time is now for us to take our fate into our own hands."

Perhaps unconvinced, or perhaps driven by other thoughts, Thargoz shook his head. "I shall not leave you. Let Oyana be the spear cast by the First Hand; it shall not be me." His eyes made plain he would not be deterred from this; this is what his heart had told him must be, and so, as Kumza would have it, Yaletha accepted it.

All three turned to Jemik, who had been strangely silent. There was a battle going on within him, and it was plain on his face. He started to speak, and stopped, and started again, but no words came out. Before he could find something to say, he was spared by the sudden sound of footsteps coming from both sides. Alertly, Thargoz and Oyana both took up their spears and turned to meet the danger. From above them, coming down the hill, was a group of six, no, eight, Oritheri, clearly meaning to capture or kill them. Axes and spears were at the ready. But from below, two dozen Haebinnor had seen their approach and were charging up to meet them; they might have been unprepared for a war, but they were certainly ready to defend the First Hand.

It was a brief battle, but a bloody one. Oyana immediately began to give orders, and when the Haebinnor seemed unsure whether to follow them, Yaletha took the opportunity to make clear that Oyana led with her blessing, as her general. The effect was immediate; no one questioned Oyana for an instant, and soon they were moving in a coordinated assault. Small groups of slaves would keep an Oritheri on the move, separating her from her fellows, until another few could overwhelm her.

When the fighting was done, four were dead, two on each side, and many more injured. Several of the Haebinnor were limping, or being carried, to Kumza's camp. But the remaining Oritheri had been disarmed and rendered helpless, being borne out to the valley to be held as prisoners of war. Their weapons and armor were being portioned out; to Yaletha's relief, none of the armor fit her slender form, though she did end up bearing a small knife. She saw the blood from the fallen and fought not to cry, but her people seemed heartened by the victory, and soon, a cheer was passing from camp to camp, heralding the First Hand. Oyana, clad in a few mismatched pieces of stolen armor, rode that wind through the valley, both rallying the people and organizing them.

Having shed his share of Oritheri blood in this battle, Jemik was breathing hard, leaning on a spear, as Yaletha stepped up to him. She looked up to catch his eye, and when he made to speak, seeing the struggle still in his eyes, she lifted a finger to his lips to silence him. "I see that you feel you ought to match every protestation of Thargoz to swear yourself by my side, but I see that, more than that, you yearn for the glory of battle, to join Oyana in becoming a part of the history of our people winning at long last their freedom." He seemed to want to protest, but she did not permit it. "You do not need to best Thargoz. Your heart tells you what you wish, what is right for you. Go, with my blessing. You will always be dear to me, but it was never really me you wanted; it was the chance to make a mark on history, to do deeds that will be sung for centuries. Today is *your* day, just as it is mine, just as it is for all of our people. Guide them to triumph." Again, he seemed to want to object, and her eyes grew stern. "I *need* you to do this," she said. "Oyana is wise and strong, but she is also cautious. There shall come a time this day when our people need your daring, your unfailing courage. Go, follow your heart."

When she finally stepped back, he stared into her eyes a few moments, then simply nodded, turned, and hurried down to join Oyana, without another word.

Thargoz and Yaletha were alone now, for the first time since the night of the First Spear, and the look they exchanged was as the full moon reflected on a wind-stirred pond. There weren't any words, and after a time they stopped waiting for any. With a breeze at their back they started up the path. Ahead, they could see the glint of armor and shining Oritheri axe-blades waiting for their necks. The prophecy offered no promises; these might well be their last moments in the world, and there was no one left to save them. But while that made her heart race with terror, that was nothing to the dread that accompanied the weight of being the First Hand. Even if they survived the road to the Spire, there would be thousands of eyes on her, thousands of souls depending on her. Fate bore down on her shoulders with the weight of mountains until she could not breathe.

When Thargoz took her hand in his, she was jolted from these thoughts. His hand was warm, and there was something in the feel of it there that seemed to say more than a thousand songs. But the road was treacherous and the wind up the hillside threatened to toss them aside; he was probably just trying to steady her climb. She swallowed and continued to pick her steps, trying to shrug off the weight of destiny. As the Spire hove back into view around the last turn in the path, and the shine of spear-points greeted her, they came to a sudden stop. It was at that moment that he turned, drew her into his arms, and kissed her. More to her surprise, she returned the kiss.

Chapter 17: Generals and Kings

By the time Jemik caught up with Oyana, the burden of being the general of the First Hand, which she'd taken up with such relish, was weighing heavily on her, enough that she welcomed his presence. Her task was almost impossibly daunting. Had she been a decorated general, well-known and respected, and had this force been made of disciplined, trained warriors who'd come ready to join this battle, there would still not have been time to organize them into an effective fighting force. But most of them did not know her, and though rumors were spreading quickly through the Haebinnor about the First Hand appointing generals, these rumors grew more muddled the farther they traveled. Not one of them was a warrior, or knew the first thing about tactics. And their determination was shaky at best; like a precariously balanced crockery jar on an overfull shelf, each of them was held up by the others, but every tremor threatened to topple and shatter them all.

Oyana had realized that her best asset was that they were, to a soul, used to taking orders and executing them without question. It made her feel a little sick to take advantage of that, but she reassured herself that, if they had to have one last mistress, better it be her than the Oritheri. The fact that many of them would be following her orders into a funeral pyre was something she tried to keep at a distance, out of her thoughts.

She was focusing her efforts on choosing lieutenants who could mobilize small groups, and captains who could carry directions to the lieutenants, when Jemik volunteered his aid. "I was starting to wonder how much longer before you would arrive," she said, to his consternation; he hadn't thought his arrival was inevitable. "I have already been instructing captains to follow your orders as they would mine. I expect the Oritheri will try to charge down our middle, counting on our lack of discipline after they've split our forces in half. You will take the side nearest the Spire, I will take the southern flank, that neither be without a leader to maintain order." She continued, talking quickly about tactics and the directives that would initiate them, leaving Jemik scrambling to keep up.

Around them, the Haebinnor were milling about, but a keen eye would recognize that there was a hint of order emerging from their movements. They were forming into small groups, and within each group, they were choosing roles. As they did, shivers of fear also coursed through the mass of people. A man might with relative calm face the prospect of battle, while it was an abstract thought, and he was surrounded by thousands of his fellows. But when he is given a specific instruction for a particular situation, he starts to absorb the very real likelihood of his injury or death, and his resolve begins to waver.

As he listened to Oyana, Jemik's eye took in the ripples in the army; he could feel their fear like the thrum in the ground when an aurochs herd is in the distance, neither seen nor heard yet, only felt. "We need to remind them of what they fight for," he said, cutting off Oyana in a discussion of contingencies. "I wish I had a horse," he muttered, then began to lope amongst the people, focusing his attention particularly on the most gregarious, those who would not just capture his enthusiasm but propagate it to others. "My people!" he shouted. "Since we were but striplings we have whispered to ourselves, every hour of every day, four words. *A day will come.* The day has come!" There was a hushed silence; across the valley, eyes were turning to him. "Today we take from the Oritheri what is our right: our freedom. Some of us may be injured. Some of us will die. But we do not fight this day for only ourselves. We fight for our children. For every man who falls today, for every woman who will not see the morrow, there shall be a hundred of our children who will walk free beneath the stars, will choose for themselves how to live, who to love, and what will come for their own families."

The more he shouted, the more ears turned to him, and now the ripples moving through the crowd were a wave of determination; people standing straighter, turning their eyes to the Oritheri with ferocity and certainty. "Our enemies think we will be meek and mewling. But tonight's moon shall rise on their end. Not one grain shall stand atop another. We have seen the signs! Five Spears have been cast! The First Hand even now moves to cry defiance to the sky itself, casting to the clouds the Sixth Spear from atop the Spire of Last Days!" He pointed to the ruined tower atop the hill, and every Haebinnor eye turned to follow. "A day will come! A day will come!" He repeated this, forming a chant that was soon taken up by the crowd, a rumble that would, if allowed, become a thunderous roar.

But the Oritheri chose this moment to move, perhaps to cut off this swell of fervor. The army let out its own scream of challenge and began to charge as one. As Oyana had foreseen, they formed a spear-tip that thrust like a splitting wedge down the middle of the Haebinnor masses, driving them apart into two flanks. And the slaves withdrew, retreating north and south, ceding the center to them with nearly no resistance.

Oyana stood atop a small rise, little more than a hillock, and peered until she could spy a man atop a horse, leading the charge. She fixed her eyes on him, and smiled. Indeed, he thought the Haebinnor were falling behind him out of fear and weakness; he was expecting an easy victory. He had not anticipated her giving directions that they allow the Oritheri to separate them. She counted the heartbeats until he and his cohort had come as far into the mass of slaves as she dared to wait, then with a few cries and gestures, she parted from Jemik, remaining with the southern flank while he took the north.

Now the Oritheri found themselves hedged in on two sides instead of a single front, but their wedge formation also separated the Haebinnor into two fronts just as effectively, and each front consisted of unarmed men and women. Finding another boulder atop which to perch, Oyana watched, expecting the bloodshed to begin in earnest any moment. But the Oritheri simply held position, waiting for something. Their advance had broken the back of Jemik's chanting; the valley was eerily silent. Even the wind slumbered while they waited. She turned to peer up the slope to the north, seeking the Spire. By now Yaletha and Thargoz should be there, raising the Sixth Spear. Every passing moment was full of dread, that they'd been captured or killed, that the Sixth Spear would never be cast, and this makeshift army's resolve would shatter unto dust. *Sand in their breath, to the end of days.*

There was a cry from amongst the Oritheri, and at once, a thousand heads turned to the southeast. There in the distance, she could barely make out a small group, not more than a dozen, riding to join her foes. The gleam of gold and silver caught the sunlight, but it was the paler shimmer of crystal that made her draw in a frightened breath. A globe of crystal, perched atop a scepter.

The Oritheri Baugcaun himself was riding to the head of his army, scepter in hand, clad in shimmering maille of brass and gold, with his personal guard around him. Gasps and whispers of despair were passing through the Haebinnor. He would not be here unless he were sure that his victory was assured; he would not put his own body in danger otherwise. Amongst the warriors of his army, there was cheering, cries, beating of spears and axe-hafts against breastplates, everywhere the tumult of blood-lust and the certainty of triumph. Some Haebinnor eyes were caught up in this spectacle, staring at it as one might stare at the axe coming for one's neck; others were cast up in mounting despair at the Spire of Last Days, where the Sixth Spear should have been seen by now.

When the Oritheri Baugcaun had taken his place at the spear-tip of his army's wedge formation, mere yards from dozens of Haebinnor, he held his scepter aloft. Sunlight kissed the crystal and cast scintillating beams of colored light, ever-shifting as the sand within the sphere danced, around him. "Your First Hand is cut off!" he shouted. "Go back to your masters now, and your punishments will be lessened. This is your final chance to avoid being ground under the heel of fate, sand in your breath."

Jemik and Oyana both bristled to hear the words of the prophecy in this Oritheri's mouth. These words, repeated so often and bearing such a weight of fear and hope, had a resonant power in the ears of every Haebinnor. Jemik had himself been using them for the same purpose minutes earlier, stirring up courage amongst the army. But that was his right as a Haebinnor. The Oritheri had taken from them everything else, their freedom, their labor, their fates, their very bodies and souls. But the prophecy, that alone, that belonged only to the Haebinnor, and the Oritheri had no rights to it.

Except, of course, it had been theirs all along, hadn't it?

Chapter 18: The Spire of Last Days

"Your last surprise was most puzzling," the Oritheri Cowr said as he stepped out from behind a piece of broken wall, only a few dozen strides from the Spire of Last Days; yet with three Oritheri warriors beside him, and more to either side, it might as well have been a hundred leagues away. "How did you arrange to have a ballista turned on my tower?"

If Yaletha or Thargoz were considering answering, they weren't given the chance; he waved his hand dismissively and continued. "It's no matter. My men have scoured this hilltop for hours. I don't know where your friends are; have they abandoned you already?" He smirked, twisting a bit of his beard with one hand. "But they aren't here, readying some surprise rescue. It is just the two of you, and the eight of us, here, waiting for you." He gestured, and more Oritheri sprung up from behind them, where they'd been hidden beside the path, ringing them completely in a circle of Oritheri. "Shall we have a cozy little chat? I'm afraid I didn't bring any tea. It seems the slaves who make it are otherwise occupied. I'm sure you'll forgive me this lapse of courtesy."

Hands still clasped together, Yaletha and Thargoz drew closer to one another. The tingle of the kiss was fading; already it seemed like a dream. She was now looking around into the shadows and hiding places afforded by the ruins. Surely her mysterious ally, the one who'd been atop the statue, had anticipated this eventuality and was already in place to rescue them? Her heart stumbled and lurched; she saw no sign of him. Nor did she know if he was an ally at all.

Gesturing to the valley beneath them, where the Oritheri army was forcing the Haebinnor masses to part before them, the Oritheri Cowr continued in a low, slippery voice. "Soon, the Oritheri Baugcaun will join his army. He and I have passed many a cheerful evening discussing this day, and it seems we have one small disagreement of strategy. The point of contention is: what shall we do with the survivors?" He turned, pontificating as if heedless of his audience, as his men tightened the circle with their spear-tips and axe-blades shining.

"There won't be many either way, I'll grant you that. But the prophecy is clear enough that they should be slain to the last. The Oritheri Baugcaun is staunchly in favor of that option. Those who surrender will be put to grisly deaths. And of course, it is ultimately his choice to make; I am but an advisor." He turned back to drink in their reaction: Thargoz was fuming, readying some passionate retort, and Yaletha was withering. Her eyes flicked side to side hoping to see some sign of the cowled figure, but this hope, and every other, was waning with every beat of her heart. She was not the First Hand, not really. It was all a deception piled atop another deception, and here, now, there was no one left to be fooled by it. Least of all her.

"You may be thinking, how could the Oritheri survive the loss of so many slaves? And this is my concern with his approach. He feels that the Haebinnor will be unruly now. If the prophecy plays out, and they are neither free nor extinct, what then? How shall we keep them in line? And he is confident that, soon, we shall have new slaves aplenty, plucked from the Sea-Lords, and new lands of conquest to pillage. Which may be true. But I feel that, even if we have Sea-Lords at our feet, they will need an example. And what better example could I offer them than the Haebinnor? You were born to be slaves. Had we not conquered you, you would have found someone else to be conquered by." As he spoke, he was striding indolently around the clearing at the base of the Spire. He paused just before Yaletha and peered deeply into her eyes. "Even now, at the verge of foment, you simper, and long for your chains."

Two of the Oritheri were right up behind them now. One held Thargoz by the upper arms, tightly enough to leave bruises, while another gripped Yaletha's shoulder just firmly enough to keep her from running, but no more. Her hand was still in his, though it was only a matter of time before they were separated. She glanced down at it, hoping to draw strength from the sight of it, but instead she saw the small knife at his side. If she moved quickly, she could snatch it and plunge it into the Oritheri Cowr's chest before anyone could stop her. He was right there, gloating, so close she could feel the breath in his words. He wouldn't have any way to avoid the blow.

And then the Oritheri would cut both of their throats. Or worse. And below them, their people would be struck down to the last. Their hope had been false all along. The prophecy was a weapon, indeed, but it was not *their* weapon; they'd been clinging to it and honing it for generations, without realizing its point was pressed against their own hearts. She was not the First Hand, and there never was such a thing as a First Hand. She looked at the knife, then turned away, her eyes darkening with shame as she knew she would not seize this moment, not make an ultimately futile and fatal gesture. That she would do nothing but be a slave.

"And this is why I believe we can still use you," the Oritheri Cowr continued after a pause. He took a half-step back, and plucked the knife from Thargoz's belt. He turned the tip to his chest and held it there; with a gesture, he urged the Oritheri holding Yaletha, who grabbed her head and turned it to face him. "Shall I take your hand and place it on the hilt myself? How else could I do more to give you this moment of opportunity? Just so that you would know, in your heart, that you lack the will to act on it. That you and your kind belong under our heels."

Her eyes flicked to Thargoz, who was still fuming, but at least had the wit to do so silently. Jemik would have thrown himself onto a spear-tip long since. Thinking of him, she turned to glance down into the valley. Even here she could see the brilliant gleam of the Oritheri Baugcaun's armor as he rode. Her people quaked before him, withering. Many were staring up at her, awaiting a sign that would never come. This final sliver of hope was about to be plucked from them and there would be nothing left.

Turning to take a few strides towards the Spire of Last Days, the Oritheri Cowr laughed, low and sinuous, like the sound of a snake over sand. "And here we are presented with the very best stage on which to show this to the last of your wretched people. I could have my men cut your hearts from your chests right now. But how much better if your people, down there," he waved a hand in an all-encompassing gesture as if to gather them all and pluck them up to put in a pouch, "see you rise into the Spire, and then, and only then, perish." He whirled to stare at her. "Do you see it? Can you see it, First Hand?"

She stared back at him blankly. If the hooded man were here, something surely would have happened by now. Perhaps this outcome was what he'd wanted all along, and he had no reason to intervene again. Perhaps the Oritheri had seized the Spire before he could position himself. For all she knew, he was lying in a ditch with an Oritheri axe in his back. There was no hope left.

"I can see that you cannot," the Oritheri Cowr continued, stepping to her and tapping her forehead. "There isn't much to you, is there? You are…" He trailed off, then laughed. "You know, I don't even know your name, or what you do. Nor does it matter. You have only one purpose left to serve. You see, back in Lithgweth it was my intent to have your death, carefully arranged, serve to reinforce the idea that the signs were false, that the sand-mouse must once more be quiet. But it will be so much more effective here, at the very cusp of your people's extermination, at this place of so much portent. These ruins are drenched in the spirit of endings. This shall be the Last Days, either of your people, or of their hope. When they, in their multitudes, see your head struck off, and the Sixth Spear fall from your lifeless hand, they will surrender. Those we allow to live will be meek and servile for a hundred generations."

At this Thargoz could be silent no more. "So, this is your plan? I can see why you are the advisor to the depraved king of a corrupt people, if you have no more idea now than to repeat your failure. It cannot work. How would they believe that they can still hope for liberation in some distant future? The prophecy is spent. There is no way they can believe that the Oritheri do not know of it. They have nothing to lose by fighting."

Stroking his beard, the Oritheri Cowr turned to Thargoz and studied him throughout this outburst. "You may be right," he conceded. "Your words echo those of the… 'depraved king of a corrupt people'; perhaps you and he have much in common. But you see, this suits my purposes just as well." He turned to gaze out over the pastures below. "Some few of your people may surrender and be spared, to become model slaves, preparing the way for their Sea-Lord successors. Perhaps some of the fellows who've abandoned you will be amongst them?" He smirked, catching Yaletha's eye, hoping this would wound her, but when it did not, he shrugged and continued. "And most will be slain. Either way, they will trouble us no more." He turned and concluded triumphantly, "All that now remains to be seen is how many choose the chain, and how many the axe."

Taking a step towards Thargoz, he spoke instead to Yaletha without turning his eyes to her. "You, the First Hand, shall be instrumental in this effort. But this slave, he is of no value to us." He then turned and stepped away. "Kill him now."

Chapter 19: A Day Will Come

After word had spread about the little healing camp Kumza had set up, a half-dozen other Haebinnor with talents in the healing arts had found their way to it. There were also a few around its edges; those who felt capable of protecting the camp, but not of going to war. Leading them was an older man who used to be a pit-fighter, scrabbling with other slaves to entertain a now-dead mistress, and thus knew a bit about bare-knuckles fighting. The years had not been kind to him, and he didn't feel like he could move quickly enough to join the battle, but he could gather other men and women around to defend the camp, should the Oritheri reach this far.

It didn't seem likely, though, as they were at the rear end of what passed for the Haebinnor army. Standing atop a fallen log, Kumza could barely make out what was going on. Another day she might climb onto Ulgi's shoulders, and if she asked right then, he'd stand and heft her up there, but he was too injured to sustain this, and needed to rest. She craned her neck toward the Spire of Last Days, barely visible from here, but there was still no movement. Still no Sixth Spear.

She could hear a raucous sound from the Oritheri, starting from the spear-point where the Oritheri Baugcaun now was plainly visible, as his horse kept him well above the others. With no injuries to treat, and growing sick with worry for her friends, she scrambled around to find a tree she could climb up into.

The Oritheri were beating their weapons against their chests, making an echoing boom, strident and threatening, drowning out everything else. Many of the Haebinnor were moving, unthinkingly, backwards from the Oritheri warriors. At the edges of the horde, she saw some moving as if to leave, to return to Lithgweth, or wherever else they'd come from. Their morale was being tattered and might break at any moment.

Then a movement caught her eye. At the fringe of the Oritheri wedge, just a few dozen strides behind the Otheri Baugcaun himself, a small group of Haebinnor rushed the mounted Oritheri. At first she thought they were attacking the horses, and her heart lurched at the idea of these poor, noble beasts being harmed by her own kind. Even at the precipice of war, when men and women would soon be spilling one another's blood, she couldn't bear the idea of an innocent horse, which had not chosen to be here, being harmed.

But while the feint and attack were directed at the horses, it was not to harm them, just to spook them. Jemik had found a slave who had served, as Yaletha had, in the horse-fields of his master. These war-horses were well-trained, but most of the training was done by the slaves, not the warriors that rode them. If he got close enough, the slave that trained the horses could give them directions that the riders could not prevent, and indeed, this was the thrust of their gambit. One, then two, then several more horses were now cavorting in careening circles, jostling their riders and casting their formation into chaos. There was a flurry of limbs and movement, sand and dust kicked into the air. And then, riding out of it, was Jemik, perched triumphantly atop a horse of roan hide, a proud beast prancing as if on parade. Dust was settling on the horse's unseated rider, lying face-down, then rising slowly under the weight of his armor.

Jemik urged the horse back into the Haebinnor ranks and let out a long holler, then a shout she could hear from here: "A day will come!" The call was, as it had been a few minutes earlier, taken up and repeated by thousands of Haebinnor, along with ragged cheers at the success of his audacious raid. He turned in circles, his horse prancing and flicking its tail, shouting. Kumza could see would-be deserters returning and taking up the chant. Soon, the sound of the Oritheri weapons being beaten against their chests was drowned out by the chant. Even iron axe-hafts beaten on steel breastplates couldn't drown out voices when they were outnumbered more than five-fold.

Taking advantage of this distraction, Oyana repeated the same gambit on the other flank, and soon she was also astride a stallion, a great beast of chestnut brown that was nearly as tall at the shoulders as was the steed of the Oritheri Baugcaun. The roaring of the Haebinnor became even more deafening.

As Kumza feared, this was too much provocation; the Oritheri Baugcaun waved his scepter, and all at once, the battle was engaged.

She had become a healer because she could do nothing else; the pain of others washed over her and she could only try to ease it, or be overwhelmed by it. But the sudden gust of fear and agony that struck her nearly made her fall from the tree. For a few long moments she could do nothing but watch, horror-struck, as axes hewed Haebinnor flesh, spears were thrust through olive-skinned bodies, and arrows were cast into the air to rain both terror and death on those who didn't chance to be on the front lines. Through the ranks, hundreds were so consumed by terror they were turning to flee, sometimes stampeding over one another. The Oritheri bellowed their battle-rage so loudly Kumza imagined the Sea-Lords might be able to hear it, that a thousand leagues away they were aquake with fear at the promise of blood.

But on each side, Oyana and Jemik were shouting orders, their horses never standing still, and groups of slaves were moving to pull Oritheri down. Without weapons, they could do little. But if four Haebinnor swarmed an Oritheri, moving together, they could knock the warrior to the ground. Several would be injured, but the Oritheri would be disarmed and trapped. As she watched this, Kumza realized, with a combination of horror and admiration, that this same tactic was being used over and over, up and down both flanks. Two or three Haebinnor would be killed, or at least injured enough to retire the battlefield, for each Oritheri, but this caused a flow of weapons and armor to be seized and put to use. This was clearly Oyana's scheme, though Jemik, to his credit, wasn't second-guessing her but directing his lieutenants to use the same tactic, while keeping up a steady stream of chants and jeers to keep up spirits. And little by little, the Haebinnor were being whittled away, but becoming better armed. Like cutting away the wood at the end of a shaft to make a sharp spear-tip.

The injured were now beginning to flow into her camp, threatening to outpace the number of healers. Someone would need to select those in most need, a hard choice for any healer, and doubly so for her. After all, one might have to pass over someone in great agony to focus on one with a lesser hurt who could be saved, but that didn't stop the pain from thrusting itself into her senses. She was just about to jump down from the tree branch to begin sorting the injured, as she caught a glimpse of Jemik, leading a dozen Haebinnor in a wild strike against the Oritheri Baugcaun himself.

But the warriors around him kept a tight circle, and Jemik was pushed back, nearly losing his horse. Several slaves were injured or killed, but she could feel, even from this far, that the Oritheri Baugcaun's arrogant confidence had been struck, even if he had not himself. He hadn't expected to be threatened at all, not even a threat so easily brushed aside. His personal guard started to work their way back into the thick of the Oritheri forces, to better protect him.

And on the flanks, the Oritheri were starting to wise up to Oyana's tactic. They paired up, one with a spear keeping the Haebinnor at bay from another with an axe. While the slaves might be willing to sacrifice themselves in a desperate gambit to steal some weapons, they were less so, when the gambit didn't stand much chance of success. The chanting was fading; more and more eyes were cast to the Spire of Last Days, where still, there was no movement, no signs of hope. And the Oritheri, having regrouped, were now carving away at the Haebinnor numbers, like a sandstorm slowly but inexorably peeling flesh from bone, one tiny piece at a time.

She turned one last time to peer up to the hillside. The Spire of Last Days was silent and motionless.

Chapter 20: The Sixth Spear

They didn't attempt anything as dramatic as to push Thargoz's head down onto a stump. While one of the Oritheri warriors held him, another lifted an axe to swing from the side, to disembowel him. It wouldn't be so quick, but it would be just as effective, and far bloodier. The Oritheri Cowr was standing beside Yaletha so they could both watch while it happened. He was on the edge of cackling with pleasure to see it, and see her reaction.

A sudden shout from the valley below carried up to them. "A day will come!" Yaletha recognized Jemik's fiery voice, and the answering roar was so loud, she was almost convinced she could feel it, like a gust of wind at her back. The Oritheri Cowr whirled around, seemingly in a panic, but as he made out what had transpired, his anxiety eased considerably. "One of those fools got himself a horse," he chuckled. "It will boot him little." But Yaletha could sense an undercurrent of trepidation in his voice. Even now, while he was gloating about their inevitable triumph, the Oritheri Cowr was nervous.

Her eyes swept the clearing around the Spire. Might the hooded man be present after all, and the Oritheri Cowr just bluffing, hoping she wouldn't notice? No, there was still no sign of him, and Yaletha started to feel embarrassed, foolish, for hoping he might rescue her, or save their cause, once more. Here she was, awaiting the axe that would claim the life of Thargoz while the warmth of his lips still was on hers, then lop off her neck as well, dashing the hopes of all her people; and still she waited impassively for a mysterious figure of unknown motives to intervene.

No, it can't be the threat of this unknown man that had the Oritheri Cowr on edge. Her mind raced as she turned over and over what she knew. All he'd said about the prophecy. The siege of the Sea-Lords. The first Oritheri Cowr and his intent and methods. His plans for the Haebinnor now, whether they all died, or only some. She felt sure there was something she wasn't grasping, but it eluded her.

The Oritheri warriors were standing still, waiting for the Oritheri Cowr, who was still watching the battlefield. It seemed Thargoz had a brief reprieve, while the Oritheri Cowr was too caught up in observing the battle to watch and enjoy the disemboweling.

Yaletha followed his eyes to the battlefield. There were both horrors and wonders there. Haebinnor being cut down by the hundreds. Throwing themselves into almost certain death merely to gain, for a moment, a bit of ground for one of their fellows, or a broken spear-haft. She swooned to think of it, being there amongst them, having to make the same terrible choice, to charge against a warrior with nothing but hope to protect her. She knew she had neither the strength nor the courage to do what these men and women were doing below her, by the hundreds, by the thousands.

Hope. That was what the prophecy had always been about. She remembered something the Oritheri Cowr had said, in his tower in Lithgweth. That hope itself had been fashioned into a weapon the Oritheri used to subjugate the Haebinnor. The Spears had given each of those brave men and women in the valley a tenuous grasp on hope, a chance to turn it back on the Oritheri, but it kept slipping away from them, lost in a haze of uncertainty.

But today, mere yards from here, within her grasp, was the means to finally seize hope, steal it from the Oritheri and turn it against them, for every Haebinnor below her. At the cost of her life, and that of Thargoz, of course. They would be cut down as a matter of course, and would have no chance to escape that fate. But for that price, she could purchase hope for her people. And that, she now saw clearly for the first time, was enough.

Suddenly, she laughed. The Oritheri Cowr turned to stare at her, as did the warriors. It was a most incongruous laugh. "What amuses you, girl?" he asked with a raised eyebrow.

"It's your own weapon," she said in between fits of giggles, "your own weapon. You fashioned it with your own hands. It seems right, somehow." Still chuckling, she whirled, one elbow connecting with

116

the ribs of the Oritheri Cowr, mostly by accident. Perched near the edge of the long drop to the valley below, he began to flail, his arms spinning. She didn't wait to see what happened; she didn't dare to catch a glimpse of an axe biting into Thargoz, spilling his guts onto the sandy stones, for fear it might strip away this sudden rush of resolve. Snatching a spear from the hand of a stunned Oritheri, she turned to run, with the fleet feet that had carried her away from so many other confrontations. In but a few moments she'd closed the distance to the Spire of Last Days and hurled herself behind the shelter of its stones. Spears shattered against the tower's wall as she scrambled up the winding stair within it.

By time she reached the peak, she could hear pursuers below her, scuffling, grunting to catch up despite their heavy armor. But she didn't dare pay them any heed. There was only one thing left in all the world for her to do; then she could meet her end, knowing that, whatever else she'd done, she'd seized, stolen, the hope of the Oritheri and made it her own. As she emerged into the sunlight, in the corner of her eye she caught a glimpse of a shape plummeting down the side of the cliff, a cloak billowing in the wind and failing to slow the fall; but she paid no heed.

She seized the spear at its center, stood tall atop the Spire of Last Days, and cried out, as loud as her voice could carry, "Hope is ours!" as she hefted the spear above her head.

Below her, arrayed across a swath of uneven pastureland, two armies paused and looked up at her. Thousands upon thousands of eyes were fixed upon her. Nothing and no one moved, not even the wind.

She tossed the spear to the clouds. Then, the winds whipping her hair around her, she turned and stepped down to meet the men coming up to murder her.

Chapter 21: Rent By The Sky

In the now-silent valley, most eyes were fixed on the Sixth Spear. There, against the clouds wheeling their way across the azure, a small figure could be seen. Thin, slight; the sort most of the Oritheri, and many of the Haebinnor, would overlook. But now, perched at the peak of the Spire of Last Days, a spear held above her, she was also the greatest of them all. "Hope is ours!" she shouted, and the Haebinnor roared.

Hardly anyone noticed a small shape, his cloak fluttering in the breeze, plunging down the rocky cliff-side, bouncing wetly across some of its jagged rocks, and ultimately vanishing behind some of them. No one would find what was left of him, save perhaps carrion-birds seeking a place to roost.

Matching Yaletha's shout, Jemik wheeled his horse around. He'd been punctuating the battle with his four-word chant, but raising a broken axe-handle towards the silhouette of the Spire of Last Days, he cried out, "Hope is ours!" By the time the Haebinnor were chanting with him, and surging back towards the Oritheri line like a sandstorm, unstoppable, Yaletha had cast the spear and vanished once more into the Spire.

Oyana's eyes were fixed not upon the hillside. She'd seen enough to know that Yaletha was alive, and also, that she would likely not be for long. But if the First Hand had done her part; now it was time for Oyana to do hers. Her eyes sought and found the Oritheri Baugcaun with the intensity of a hunting lynx peering at a juicy sand-mouse. She watched as gust after gust of Haebinnor hurled themselves against the Oritheri forces, scattering them, at terrible cost. Countless Haebinnor would go to Kumza's camp, and more would go nowhere but into the thirsty sand. The Oritheri warriors were not daunted; their unquenchable battle rage roiled within them. But each warrior, lost in her own rage, screamed and fought heedless of the others. Their discipline had fled, drowned out by the chanting and roars, and now they battled, oblivious of their own fellows, their formations, their very purpose.

The moment approached. She held perfectly still, in the midst of the storm, and waited. Soon. Soon.

Now.

She spurred her horse forward and plunged through a gap in the Oritheri guards. At the last moment the Oritheri Baugcaun whirled and saw her coming. He threw himself aside, avoiding the death blow he expected was reaching for him, and rolled on the sand. Then slowly he rose, smirking. She'd come for him, she'd taken her moment, and she'd failed. He was unharmed.

He turned to gloat at her, and then stopped in his tracks. There she sat atop the mighty chestnut steed, and her eyes were on his. She had an unsettling smile.

And in her hand, she held his scepter.

He reached out a hand impotently towards her and cried, "No!" but he could do nothing as she held it aloft, then with one hand, crushed the crystal sphere.

He whirled around once more, but by the time his eyes found Lithgweth, the spectacle was nearly done. Sand was trickling down through Oyana's fingers, and there, on the horizon, the city was blowing away. It didn't burst, or shatter. There were no tumbling stones; the ground did not shake. There was no sound, save a thin whistling of the wind.

The city simply blew away. As if it had been a mere momentary happenstance, grains of sand moving and aligning for a split second in the shape of a city; and in the next moment, each grain of sand had its own idea of where to go, and the city was no more. As if it had never been.

"Their works rent by the sky until not one grain stands atop another," Oyana remarked dryly. Then almost as an afterthought, she spurred the horse forward, snatched up an axe, and lopped off the gape-mouthed head of the Oritheri Baugcaun. She raised the head to the

sky, so that every man and woman, every warrior and slave, could see it. "*None shall mourn them*," she shouted, over the stunned silence that suddenly surrounded her.

Chapter 22: False Signs

The first to reach the Spire was not an Oritheri warrior, hungry for Yaletha's blood, but Thargoz. He'd managed to slip out of their grasp in the confusion, and, like Yaletha, could close the distance to the Spire faster than his armor-clad enemies. But only a little; they were right behind him. When he met her at its base, he turned and stood, sheltering her with his body. "Run," he whispered. "Perhaps you can get away while they finish me."

But she had accepted her fate. She had done what she came for. She wanted nothing more than to be with him now. She put her arms around him from behind and waited for the moment, her eyes closed.

When it hadn't come a few moments later, she opened them once more and peered around him. In a circle around them, the Oritheri had paused, staring into the distance, down into the valley. She turned to follow their gaze, still embracing Thargoz, and for a few moments, eyes wide, she watched as Lithgweth was swept away, erased as if it had never been. There was a gasp from the warriors, and she soon found its cause: Oyana's cry, holding aloft the severed head of the Oritheri Baugcaun.

She turned to meet the eyes of the warriors, and they fixed theirs on her. She could almost feel, as if for a moment she had borrowed Kumza's gift, their thoughts and feelings. The shock of all that had been lost. The thought of turning and running now, to salvage something of their world. And the desire to wreak bloody vengeance on the First Hand. They raised their axes and spears once more, their warrior's rage winning out over the other thoughts.

And a horse charged through the ruins, scattering the warriors. A man rode atop it, shrouded in a hood and cloak the color of dried blood, his face shrouded in shadows much the same. The Oritheri warriors struggled for balance a moment, then, thinking better of it, turned to scramble back down the path to join the few of their remaining kin. The rider wheeled his horse around and turned to peer out from the shadows of his hood at Yaletha and Thargoz.

"You!" she cried. "You are the one who placed the stake atop the monument!" With a slight movement of his head, the man nodded. "And the others? Did you falsify all the Spears?"

He shook his head. "We bred a horse with markings in its hide, and sold it on a day when a sandstorm would make the moon red. We placed a tree, positioned an iron stake, and, in a moment of panic, we captured and fired a ballista. No more. Mere showmanship, sleight of hand. It was you who made the prophecy come true, you who persevered, you who understood. It was you who won your freedom this day."

Yaletha shook her head. "You called a storm! That is more than sleight of hand." But the man only grinned as if to say such things were impossible, but without denying it. Or indeed saying anything. When it was clear he would offer no response, she asked, while still clinging to Thargoz, "Who are you?"

"My name is unimportant. You shall not look upon my likeness again."

"But why? Why do all this?"

She thought she heard a chuckle. "It is a fair question," he conceded with a bow of his head. "You are not the first First Hand, Yaletha. We have attempted this many times over the years. And each time, the man or woman who chanced to be identified as the First Hand failed to take up the charge. What little was accomplished was suppressed by the Oritheri, buried, and forgotten. When we saw that you were the new First Hand, we despaired." His voice was wry but also kind. "You did not seem particularly promising. But you were to be the last First Hand, whether you succeeded or no."

She gaped at him. "Why was I to be the last?"

He turned and gazed into the setting sun. "Far from here, great events of which you know little are taking place. Half the Oritheri army marches now to a battle in a distant land. We had hoped an earlier attempt would cause the Oritheri to be defeated before they could send *any* forces to that battle. Other efforts of ours have prevented the march of many other tribes into the lands of the Sea-Lords. But at least we've halved how many Oritheri soldiers now lay siege to the Great City."

Yaletha had never heard of a Great City. Her thoughts went to Lithgweth, the greatest city she'd ever heard of, but it was gone, and in any case, clearly not what the mysterious man meant. "So this was all to save some Sea-Lord princeling?" she asked, momentarily angry.

He turned back to fix his eyes on her. "Yes, and no," he said, apparently amused by her ire. "We certainly wished to help turn the tide of a battle of which you know nothing; it is what set us on this road. A terrible shadow will rise and, hopefully, fall, without you even knowing what horror you have been spared. No, more than spared. That you have helped to spare yourself. But we did not engage in this action merely for them. If we had found that, to save the, as you call it, Sea-Lord princeling, we had to enslave your people rather than help them free themselves, we would have sought another way. Or at the last, we would have turned away. No victory won through embracing darkness can ever stay true, can ever strike down darkness."

"You speak as if you care about us," she said, though the anger was ebbing. Thargoz's hand was warm in hers. "You used us just as much as the Oritheri did." But she regretted the words as soon as she'd said them.

Unperturbed, the man simply shrugged. "As I said, all we did was play a few pranks. It was you who found hope in the sand, who had the strength to hold it aloft, who struck down your oppressors and found your own way. It is this, not some distant war, that you should hold in your thoughts this day."

127

"What do we do now?" Yaletha asked.

"That is, for the first time, no one's to decide but your own," the man said, turning his horse to the path. "A new life stands open before you. Make of it something the equal of what you have done today, and your name will be sung a thousand years from now." He spurred his horse into motion, and soon disappeared around the stones of the hill.

Without another word, Yaletha tugged Thargoz's hand, and began the slow descent to meet their fellows. There was a new life to discover, and much work to be done.

Made in the USA
Middletown, DE
17 October 2024